THE WAY
HOME
LOOKS
NOW

Also by Wendy Wan-Long Shang
THE GREAT WALL OF LUCY WU

THE WAY HOME LOOKS NOW

WENDY WAN-LONG SHANG

SCHOLASTIC INC.

Copyright © 2015 by Wendy Wan-Long Shang

This book was originally published in hardcover by Scholastic Press in 2015.

All rights reserved. Published by Scholastic Inc., *Publishers since 1920*. SCHOLASTIC and associated logos are trademarks and/or registered trademarks of Scholastic Inc.

ISBN 978-0-545-60957-9

10 9 8 7 6 5 4 3 2 1   17 18 19 20 21

Printed in the U.S.A.   40
First printing 2017
Book design by Abby Kuperstock

For my father and brother

PEOPLE ASK ME WHAT I DO IN WINTER
WHEN THERE'S NO BASEBALL. I'LL TELL YOU WHAT I DO.
I STARE OUT THE WINDOW AND WAIT FOR SPRING.

—ROGERS HORNSBY

• CHAPTER •
ONE

I AM ONLY GONE LONG ENOUGH TO GET THE EGGS.

Ba had asked me to stop by the Minute Mart after school, but I had forgotten and come straight home, only to have to leave again. I ride my bike, but with the eggs I have to ride fast-slow—slow enough that the eggs won't break but fast enough that I won't get in trouble. When I turn the corner to our street, I see my sister, Elaine, sitting on the steps. She had been inside when I left, but now she is outside, holding her binoculars.

"What are you doing, Laney? Looking for birds?" Laney usually looks for birds in the morning, but really, for her, anytime is a good time.

I move past her to open the door. The knob turns slightly but then stops hard.

"We're locked out?" I ask, trying to make it sound like it's not a big deal.

Elaine draws a quick, sharp breath of air. "I came outside to get my binoculars. I knocked but . . ." She stops.

"Do you think you locked the door on your way out? Or did the door lock behind you after you left?" I say the words a little more harshly than I mean to.

"I don't know." Now, for the first time, Elaine looks frightened. "I knocked and rang the doorbell, but I guess she didn't hear me."

I pound on the door, hard enough that I can feel it all the way down to my bones. I press the doorbell, too. "Mom! Mooom!" I try all the variations, barking her name, dragging out the middle like a foghorn, standing away from the door and throwing my head back like a dog.

Nothing. Silence.

It's probably okay, I tell myself. *Elaine probably just locked the door without meaning to. Mom's probably okay. She has to be okay.* But then another voice edges in. *Shouldn't she have noticed that Elaine isn't in the house?*

I turn the doorknob a little harder, just to check, but it stays put. "Why don't you wait here for Ba," I say. I make my voice light. "I'm going to try the back door."

"Can I . . ."

"No, it's easier if you stay here," I lie. I walk slowly to the corner of the house until Elaine can't see me. And then I start running.

• • •

My legs feel heavy and dull. I can't go fast enough. The ground is wet and thick from the last of the snow. The back of the house might as well be a mile away, though I finally get there.

The kitchen door is also locked—we almost never open it in the wintertime—but there's a window, and that's all I need. If I stand in the right place, I can see through the kitchen doorway into the living room. My heart hammers against my chest, threatening to split me in two.

I don't know what I thought I was going to see, but she's there. She's still there. Mom. She's sitting on the couch, watching TV, the way she has for the last six months. From where I'm standing, it looks like the TV is making her curl and fade away, like a scrap of newspaper in the sun.

I look down at the ground and then look back up, double-checking. She is still there, inhaling, exhaling, blinking. She didn't lock us out on purpose. Elaine must have accidentally hit the lock button, and then Mom didn't hear her knocking.

I see the front door open, and Ba walks in, followed by Elaine. Elaine squeezes around him and heads for the living room.

Ba takes off his coat and carefully places it on a hanger. Then he takes off his shoes, one by one, untying the laces and putting the shoes side by side on a rug by the door. He is so slow, so careful in the way he moves. He wasn't worried about the door being locked. I imagine him pulling up in the driveway, saying hello to Elaine and then unlocking the front door. He probably doesn't even notice I am gone.

Ba disappears briefly as he walks down the hallway, behind the wall, and then he reappears at the living room doorway. He sticks his head in for just a moment, and then heads upstairs. Like nothing is wrong. Like there is nothing even close to being wrong.

Through the window, it feels like I'm watching my own TV show, except the sound is off. Just like with real TV, I can't tell the characters what to do. If I could write my own TV show, Ba would hurry inside. He would know that something is wrong when Elaine is locked out. And he wouldn't act like Mom watching TV all day is normal.

I wonder how it is that he can see so little when I see so much.

"Peter, come here," Ba calls when I come inside. I put the eggs in the refrigerator and go upstairs, to where Ba is sitting on the edge of his bed.

I'm barely in the door when he looks at me and frowns. "You're tracking in mud."

I look down, and sure enough, there is a trail of muddy footprints behind me. I reach down and pull off my shoes, one by one. In the process, I get some of the mud on my shirt.

Ba closes his eyes and shakes his head. "I got a call from Miss Gunderson before I left work today," he says. He is a pharmacist at Merkimer's Drug. "Do you know what Miss Gunderson said to me?"

Here's what my father can see: reports from teachers, bad grades, unfinished homework.

I am sure the old bat has lots to say about me, not that I'm going to offer any guesses. Ba continues, "Miss Gunderson told me that you do not write your name on your paper. Not a single assignment. And you are the only one in her English class who fails to write down his name."

Miss Gunderson seems to take my existence in her class as a personal insult. Maybe she thought she was getting a different kind of student, the kind I was last year. I wasn't the smartest, but I did okay. *A pleasure to have in class.* That kid is gone, though.

"If I'm the only one, then she should know that the paper with no name is mine," I point out.

Ba ignores my comment. "Your teacher explained to me that her rules are there to ensure an orderly classroom. And one of those rules is that you must write your name on all your papers to receive full credit." Ba pauses a moment to consider the full extent of my misdeed. "Is this some form of *rebellion*?"

"What? No." It is just like Ba to think my forgetfulness is actually a criminal act.

Ba picks up the *Pittsburgh Post-Gazette* and shows it to me, snapping the paper so it crackles. "Are you sure? Because look at this. These *high school students* had a sit-in in the cafeteria. Eight hundred of them! It's that bad influence from the colleges."

My father's disdain for the Vietnam War protestors is well known in our family.

"Tell me the truth," demands Ba. That is his other big bugaboo—being honest.

"I'm not staging a protest," I tell him. But it's too late. Ba starts his rant.

"You have one job, and that is to focus on school. *Do your best.* These students here"—he thwacks the newspaper with his hand—"they are protesting the *vending machines*. When I was a student in China, I would never have dreamed of doing such a thing. We stood up when the teacher entered the room. The teacher commanded the highest authority."

What I want to say is, *But back then, there wasn't a war in Vietnam or women fighting for equal rights. You didn't worry about getting bused to a different school because everyone in China looks the same.* My father didn't even have a TV; I'm not sure they were even invented back then. It's not the same.

When my father is satisfied that a rebellion is not imminent, he has another question. "Are you writing about the baseball players again?"

I shake my head. Last year, I wrote about baseball for every assignment I could. I wrote a haiku about laying down a bunt. My essay on a famous landmark was on Forbes Field. After managing to work in a reference to the Pirates in all my spelling word sentences, my teacher called and said that maybe I should take a break from writing about baseball for a while. But I haven't written about baseball in a long time.

You would think that my father, man of science and great believer in cleanliness and order, would love baseball. Out of all the sports, it is the most precise, the most mathematically pleasing. There are nine positions, nine innings, three strikes at bat, and three outs for each team. Baseball is so exact that it is the only sport I know of that officially assigns *errors* to players when they screw up.

Maybe after this latest run-in with Miss Gunderson, Ba would like to assign an error to me. Ba is convinced that if I just work harder, if I just stop making mistakes, I will be a great student, but the truth is, even if we get past the no-name-on-paper and unfinished homework, it's still not going to happen. But my father has enough troubles as it is without me bursting his bubble. I just hope by the time he figures things out, the disappointment won't be too hard.

Maybe by then, Mom will feel better.

On the way to dinner, I duck into the living room to check on Mom. It's dark, but it's always some kind of dark, even as the days are slowly getting longer. The only real light is from the flicker of the television.

"Hi, Mom." I don't really need to have the light on to see her. She's in the same position as when I looked through the back door. She is sitting on the far side of the couch, next to the telephone table. She has one arm across her stomach and one arm folded up so that her hand is against her cheek. I want to sit next to her, just for a moment, and pretend we live in the Before. Back then, Mom might watch TV for a few minutes before cooking dinner or while she was waiting for the timer to go off for a pie in the oven. She would put her arm around me and ask about my day. I'll tell you that I've thought about all the times I said my day was *not bad*, without really appreciating how good it was to have a not-bad kind of day.

But instead I sit near her at the end of the couch, not next to her, because we live in the After. In the After, Ba is making scrambled eggs in the kitchen. In the After, Ba yells at me if he thinks I'm bothering Mom, and I'll take anything I can from her, even a quiet moment.

Ba appears in the doorway. "Leave your mother alone, Peter. She is tired."

"Will you come eat with us tonight?" I ask her.

A commercial comes on, temporarily illuminating Mom's face. She closes her eyes and shakes her head. "I'm not hungry."

I'm disappointed, but not surprised.

"Come, Peter," says Ba, more urgently this time. I slide out of the living room, past Ba, into the harsh light of the kitchen. Elaine is already waiting at the table, tapping her fork against her plate.

"Cut it out," I tell her.

Elaine scowls at me, and then taps on her plate a few more times just to make a point. She stops when Ba walks back into the kitchen, though.

It's not a big table, but there is a lot of space for just the three of us. Sometimes Elaine or I have to get up and walk around the table to get the bottle of soy sauce that's been left too close to the far end or the milk jug that's just out of reach. It would be easier to stretch across the table, but Ba won't allow it. It's not proper. When Ba has to work on Saturdays, and Elaine and I eat lunch alone, we stretch across the table until our stomachs are in the middle and our legs are hanging off the ends. We feel like we're getting away with something, even though we're the only ones there.

Ba brings the frying pan over to the table and begins serving eggs. They tumble out of the pan, dry and rubbery. Ba adds two buttered triangles of toast to each plate. That's dinner.

There was a tiny sliver of time when the ladies in the neighborhood brought us dinners. They brought over every kind of casserole. Tuna noodle. Chicken à la king. Shepherd's pie. I think they chose those dishes because they're soft and warm, and that's what you need when you're sad.

How are you doing? they would ask, usually holding a casserole dish with two oven mitts. Their voices would be extra soft and clear. They would lean forward slightly and look down the hall. "How is your mother? Are you being a good boy for her?"

"She can't come out right now," I would repeat the words Ba had told me to say. "Thank you for asking about her."

I remember liking the dinners, the fact of them—foil-wrapped gifts. It made me feel secure to know they were there. But Ba hated them.

He couldn't bring himself to refuse, to say *no*. That would be too rude. But I could tell from the way he accepted the pans that he hated them, and not just because he likes Chinese food better than American. No matter how good the food smelled, he would never say anything but thank you. He would say the words like he was trying not to let his lips touch his teeth. The fact that those ladies showed up with their casseroles meant that they knew about us—these people who didn't really know us except for the fact that we lived on the same street. We were exposed.

Eventually, the casseroles stopped coming; that was an unspoken signal that we were supposed to go on with our lives and act like everyone else. I bet that made Ba feel better. I still miss them.

·CHAPTER·
TWO

IN THE BEFORE, HE WAS A GOD HURLING LIGHTNING bolts across the universe.

He was my brother, throwing pitches in the backyard.

"Watch me again," said Nelson. He kicked his leg high and reared back, and then fired another one. The ball skipped off the edge of my glove, crashing into the hydrangeas. The leaves shook, and the last of the dried petals fell like snow.

There was no real snow. Instead, it was that point in August when it seemed like we would always be hot and sweaty. It would never be fall; we would never have Christmas. It was only ten in the morning, and sweat was already running into my eyes, making them sting.

We were waiting to climb into our station wagon to go to the Little League World Series in Williamsport. Taiwan was in the final, playing a US team from Gary, Indiana. Every Chinese family we knew was going, and in Taiwan, where it was already nighttime, my grandparents, aunts, uncles, and cousins were napping so that they could get up later, in the middle of the night, and listen to the game on the radio.

"This is a chance for the world to remember Taiwan again," Ba had said at breakfast. This was a bitter point for him. My father's family had fled the Communist takeover of China when he was a boy. They joined other Chinese who set up the Kuomintang government in Taiwan; to him, the real China was Taiwan.

But the world seemed to be paying more attention to China, the big one. Ba said there was even talk of removing Taiwan from the United Nations in favor of China. I was not quite sure what that meant, but it didn't sound good.

In any case, I could tell this was a big deal because my father was willing to drive for three hours to watch a baseball game. Ba usually drove that far for a family event or for something he thought was *educational*, but baseball had never fit that category before. Maybe he thought this game would be instructive or informative or one of those other good-for-you words.

But for me and Nelson, with or without the politics, it was exciting because it was *baseball*. And while we were waiting to leave, Nelson suddenly got it into his head that I needed to know how to throw a palmball.

If Nelson said I needed to know something, I believed him. Nelson taught me everything I knew about baseball. Nelson was the one who taught me how to read from the sports page and took me to the batting cage. When I was five, I would tell anyone who would listen that the first commissioner of baseball was the oddly named Kenesaw Mountain Landis. But the most important thing Nelson taught me was that the Pittsburgh Pirates were the best team in the world. Even though I was just a baby when Bill Mazeroski hit his walk-off home run to win the '60 Series in the ninth inning of the seventh game, I always felt like I had been there because Nelson saw it. He told me about it, over and over, like a fairy tale.

"Make a split between your ring and middle fingers," said Nelson. "Hold it deep in your hand." Everything came easily to him: sports, grades, even girls. He was the *lao da*, the oldest, the most important. The firstborn son. He never played on the high school team, though, which everyone said was a shame. Ba said school came first.

Nelson walked to the other end of the yard, squatted down, and held up his glove. "Don't overthink it. Just throw it."

I gripped the ball the way Nelson showed me, and

wound up. Even though I understood, in theory, how it all worked, in some ways it seemed more like magic than science that you could change the spin and direction of this little ball just by changing the grip, the way the air traveled over the seams.

"Not a bad first try, Peter," said Nelson. He tossed the ball back to me. "Try again."

I wound up, and then stopped. "The Pirates have a game today," I said to Nelson. I wasn't telling him because he didn't know. Of course he knew. I was really trying to say something else.

Nelson shook his head. "Can't put the nut on too soon. It won't work if you start too soon."

This was our ritual, our magic: putting a peanut, exactly one peanut still in its shell, on the radio, for the Pirates. I don't even remember why, exactly, a peanut ended up on the radio, but I do know it happened for the first time during Dock Ellis's no-hitter, and we'd done it ever since. It didn't always work, but we'd reached the point that *not* putting a peanut on the radio seemed downright dangerous. As Nelson said, we had to show that we believed.

I was in the middle of another windup when I heard the squeak of the back door opening.

"Peter, have you packed your homework? And, Nelson, you should help your mother get ready."

I hung my head. I was the only kid I knew who had to do homework over the summer. Three pages in a workbook, Monday through Friday. Laney had homework, too, but hers was so easy it didn't really count. This was all Ba's idea.

Nelson tried to help me out. "Hey, Ba, why don't you give Peter a break today? Today is kinda special."

There are silences from people who just have nothing to say, and silences from people who say everything by ignoring you. My father had perfected the latter.

"I'll get it," I said, a little too loud. "It's no big deal." My father and Nelson had been fighting all summer—over every topic they could think of. That morning, they had fought over Nelson's hair, which Ba said was too long, and which I thought made him look kind of like Bruce Lee, the kung fu movie star. Nelson probably couldn't wait to go back to college. Most of the fights were Ba's fault; our appearance, our grades, our behavior—no matter how good—were never good *enough*. Laney caught some slack, because she was the youngest and a girl, but that just meant Ba had more energy for me and Nelson.

When I came back outside, Mom and Nelson were loading our orange cooler into the back of the station wagon. I could hear the glass soda bottles clinking inside.

"What did you pack?" I asked.

Mom ticked the items on her fingers. "Fried chicken, potato salad, strawberries, and a cake." And then, knowing what my next question would be, she added, "Lemon chiffon cake."

I should have known she had made a cake because the mixer kept messing up the TV reception last night. Mom always knew the right thing to cook. Lemon cake tartness would cut right through a hot summer day.

"Hey, Peter," said Mom. She reached into her apron pocket and pulled out a peanut. She blew on it and rubbed it between her hands. "Don't forget this before we leave." She tossed it to me. Mom loved the Pirates as much as we did, and had burned more than one shirt getting caught up in listening to a game on the radio while she ironed. Her favorite player was Roberto Clemente. Mom liked to say he was a great player and a true gentleman.

"We need to get going," said Ba, locking the front door. "We need to make sure we are there before the game starts." He turned the knob, testing it.

"Wait," I said. "I need to go back inside."

Ba sighed. "I already told you to use the bathroom."

"It will take just a second," I pleaded. I tucked the peanut inside my fist. Ba didn't know about the peanut, and more to the point, he wouldn't care.

Ba looked at Mom, and Mom smiled and made a motion with her head. *C'mon. Let him in.* Ba turned the key and opened the door a crack. I dashed in before he could change his mind.

When I came back out, Mom and Ba got into the front seat. Then Nelson climbed in the row behind them. I bowed low and pointed to the car. "After you, Lady Elaine," I said, all gentlemanlike.

Elaine crossed her arms. "Oh no. I'm not falling for that. You just want me to sit in the middle!"

"I am distressed," I said, putting my hands over my heart. "Dismayed by your very accusation!" Elaine was, however, also correct. I hated sitting in the middle of the station wagon. You didn't get a window, and there was a hump on the floor in front of the middle seat that was too narrow to put both feet on top and too wide to comfortably put one foot on each side.

"Children." Ba folded his arms. Elaine and I stared at each other, neither one of us willing to budge.

"C'mon, Peter. Sit next to me. I'll help you with your homework," said Nelson. I got in first, and then Elaine, who smiled like a priss.

I waited as long as I could, telling Ba that doing homework on the side streets made me carsick. He didn't argue with me about that. Once we were on the highway, though, Ba told me to take out my workbook.

I had to do a page of long division with decimals problems, something we had covered in fifth grade. I wouldn't say *learned*, because that wouldn't be accurate. I was there, present in the classroom when it was taught. But it didn't sink in. I would say thumbscrews, hot coals, and long division with decimals were all forms of torture. I never got that dumb little dot in the right place.

"Who needs it?" I asked when I checked the answers in the back of the workbook and discovered I hadn't gotten a single answer right so far. I shut the workbook and tried not to think about throwing it out the window. It probably would have looked like a bird, its white pages flapping in the wind.

"Here," said Ba. "Give it to me." He drove with one hand and wrote with the other, using the dashboard as a desk. "Do it this way." He handed it back.

I shook my head. "That's not the way my teacher taught it."

Ba looked at me in the rearview mirror. "This is the way I learned it."

"This is American math, not Chinese math." Ba didn't know anything about being a kid in America. I constantly had to explain my life to him: slumber parties, tree houses, professional football. Once, on my sixth birthday, I was about to blow out the candles when Ba stopped everything.

"What does this mean, 'Make a wish'?" he asked. He'd heard it before, of course, but it was like he was hearing it for the first time.

We told him that it was just for fun. A birthday custom. Ba made a face and sighed. Children should say "I will work" when they want to say "I wish," he said. I will work for a new baseball glove. I will work for a new Frisbee. I knew what he was thinking: We were spoiled. Spoiled American children. Now my father sighed again, no doubt thinking that my lack of enthusiasm for long division was another sign of how spoiled and lazy I was. "Peter, mathematics is an international language. A right answer is a right answer."

I looked at the way my father had set up the problem. I felt more confused than ever.

"Try it," insisted Ba, and the pressure in his voice made me tense up.

"Hey, hey, hey. What's going on here?" Nelson slid the workbook away from me and looked at it. "Long division! With decimals! Cool." The wind whipped his hair into his eyes.

"You don't really . . ." my father started.

Nelson leaned over so I could hear him better. "You know, if you really like baseball, you should like long division, *especially* with decimals," Nelson continued.

"Long division has nothing to do with baseball," I said. "Baseball is *fun*."

"What was Clemente's average last year?" asked Nelson. He grinned. I tapped my cheek, pretending to think, but we both knew what was coming.

"Three fifty-two," announced Mom from the front seat. "And he was a Gold Glove, *again*."

"We *say* three fifty-two, but of course, it's really . . ." Nelson wrote imaginary numbers in the air.

"*Point* three five two," I finished for him. I hadn't thought of it that way. "Because you divide the number of hits by . . ."

". . . the number of at bats." Nelson finished my sentence. "Right?"

"And you can't get a number greater than one because that would mean the player got more hits than at bats." Nelson slid my pencil to the left. "So the decimal goes *there*. Remember, you can always move the decimal point two spots to the right, and that's the same as the percentage. Clemente was hitting 35.2 percent last year, or about one out of three at bats."

Suddenly it all came together. "Yeah! Okay!" I looked at the problem again, and now the numbers seemed to snap to attention. It was easier if I approximated the answer first. "I see it now!"

Mom turned around in her seat. "That was a good idea, Nelson."

"Peter could have solved it the other way," said Ba.

"But this way, he understands it better," said Nelson. Nelson was right, of course. He understood how I thought.

Ba made a noise in his throat. It sounded like the first rumble of a thunderstorm.

Please don't fight, I begged silently. Ba had just said all the answers were the same, but of course, he didn't listen to himself.

Mom made a clucking noise in her throat. "Hey," she said, trying to change the subject. "Who thinks Taiwan is going to win again?" Taiwan had won its first Little League World Series two years ago, stunning everybody including the regular Far East champion, Japan. We didn't talk about anything else for a week; not even school.

"Me," we all said together. This we could agree on. Then Elaine piped in, "But it'd be okay if the US won, too."

"It's more important for Taiwan than the US," said my father.

"It's also a baseball game," said Nelson, half joking.

"If Taiwan wins this most American of games, the US must pay attention to Taiwan, not just China," said Ba, not getting the joke.

"Did you read about that kid on the other team?" said Mom. "What's his name? McClendon?"

"Yeah, they're starting to call him Legendary Lloyd. And he's had four home runs so far in the tournament," I said. Nelson nodded.

"He's also their pitcher," said Mom. "He's had a shut-out, too."

I couldn't believe these players were my age. They were going to be on TV, playing for the right to be *world champions*.

Ba pointed at my workbook. "Finish your work, Peter. I'll check it when you're done."

• • •

There is a steep hill down to the Howard J. Lamade Stadium, which makes it look like a stage, with the hills and sky behind it a perfect backdrop. You need tickets to sit in the bleachers, but you can sit on the grassy hill beyond the outfield for free. That's where we sat, along with what seemed like every other Chinese person on the East Coast.

Mom spread out a blanket for us to sit on. A man walked by and gave us little flags for Taiwan. Taiwan's colors are also red, white, and blue—a solid red field with a blue rectangle with a white sun in the upper left-hand corner. Elaine found a US flag, too, and waved both while she ran around.

"You should really just pick one side," I told her.

Laney shook her head. "I don't want anyone to feel bad," she told me. Then she skipped away.

Mom and Ba talked to the other Chinese families sitting on nearby blankets. Mom reported that the coach for Taiwan had announced that he would rather lose with honor than intentionally walk McClendon. I also overheard some of the families talk about *hei ren*, black people. The newspapers had said that the team from Gary was the first all-black team to play in the championships. Most of the players from Taiwan, I guessed, had probably never seen a black person up close before, and it was probably vice versa for the players from Gary.

The US team jumped out to a three-run lead in the first inning when McClendon hit a long ball for a homer that drove in two other runners. He didn't even look like he was swinging hard—he was that good. My father put his hands over his head and groaned.

We were in the middle of a scoreless second inning when a pair of legs interrupted my view.

"Hiiii, Peter," said the legs. It was Clarissa Liao. Her mom and dad, who I called Liao *Ai Yi* and Liao *Su Su*, were my parents' best friends. Clarissa was good friends with Elaine, even though she was closer to my age.

"Do you mind not blocking my view?" I asked. I couldn't just shove her to one side because my parents were there. She probably knew that, too. At least she was skinny enough that she couldn't block the entire game. I could still see home plate.

"Yech, you actually care about this game? It's boring." She flopped down next to me and sat too close on purpose. Her bony shoulder pressed against me. I scooted away.

"Actually, I do. And what's that smell? Are you wearing bug spray?" I waved my hand in front of my face.

"It's a new perfume. My mom bought it from our neighbor who is an Avon lady. It's called Firefly." She flipped her hair over her shoulder and almost hit me in the eye.

"Rest assured, it smells *exactly* like fireflies," I told her. "Dead ones."

"Why, you, oh!" Clarissa sputtered. She jumped up and stomped back to her own blanket. Elaine followed her, and they began whispering and giggling.

I went back to watching the game, swatting at the gnats. I hadn't noticed them before, so maybe Clarissa's perfume was really a bug *attractor*.

Nelson leaned over. "You know she likes you, right, Peter?"

"Who?"

"Clarissa. That's why she came over here." Nelson looked over his shoulder. "She's kind of cute, you know."

I took a quick peek at Clarissa. "I suppose if you like long black hair, big bug eyes, and stinky perfume, she's not so bad." Girls were completely mysterious to me. They traveled in packs, and they spent lots of time talking behind cupped hands.

Nelson laughed. "When you're my age, you'll understand."

"If she had a Chinese Taipei jersey, then we could talk," I said.

The coach from Taiwan decided to reconsider his promise not to intentionally walk McClendon. Then Taiwan tied things up in the fourth inning when a run came in on a wild overthrow. It was anyone's game now. There were two more innings to go in regulation. Ba cupped his hands over his mouth and shouted, "*Jia you!*" which made me jump. My father never shouted in public, but he was joining the Taiwan fans. *Jia you* meant "add gas" or "go!"

The game stretched beyond the regulation six innings. Mom opened the cooler and began putting together paper plates full of food, serving Ba first. I could barely eat. I nibbled at the chicken, and then looked over Nelson's shoulder. He was scoring the game. The batter struck out looking; Nelson wrote in a backwards K.

"I never go down looking," I said.

"It happens," said Nelson. "It's happened to me. You get fooled sometimes."

"Nothing worse than getting caught flat-footed, right? That's why you score it differently from the guy who was at least swinging away."

"You're doing your job, the pitcher is doing his job. That's all."

I supposed. There were lots of guys going down at the plate. McClendon and Taiwan's pitcher, Chin-Mu Hsu, battled from the mound. Hsu threw strikeout after strikeout.

The crowd grew louder. We all chanted together:

Hsu Chin-Mu	Chin-Mu Hsu
Bie huang	Don't be afraid
Bie ji	Don't be nervous
Jiu hao hao tou qiu	Just keep pitching well

Seventh inning. Eighth inning. We ate the lemon cake and finished off our Cokes.

"They're both good teams," said Mom, stretching her arms. "It's just a matter of who is going to last longer." It didn't seem fair that the Taiwan team could lose; they had to fly halfway around the world to come play. If they lost, they would have that whole long flight back home to stew about it. And I didn't even want to think about what Ba would do if they lost. I stared at the game and tried to will the team to play better.

Finally, in the ninth inning, Taiwan broke loose. They scored *nine* runs in a collection of hits, bunts, and bad throws from the US team. Even from far away in the field, I could see McClendon lower his head and begin to sob, his shoulders shaking. His coach walked over, put his arm around him, and led him off the mound. I felt kind of bad for him, but at the same time, the United States would need a miracle to win at this point.

As the home team, the US team had the last at bat, but they couldn't score. When the ump called the last strike, the crowd broke open into the loudest roar I had ever heard. It sounded like the ocean, with no beginning or end. Nelson cupped his hands around his mouth and joined them, so I did, too, our voices blending into the sound.

Mom and Ba shook hands with all the Chinese fans who sat near us. Clarissa tried to give me a hug, but I managed to duck away at the last minute by pretending I needed to tie my shoe.

It took a while for us to make our way back to the station wagon. By then, it was getting dark, and the real fireflies were starting to come out. Mom rested her head on Ba's shoulder and looked at us right before we got in the car. "What a perfect day with our family," she said. "That was some game." She looked pleased, as though all of this had happened just for us.

"It is a good day for Taiwan," said Ba.

"It was going to be a good day either way, because we're Chinese *and* American. Right?" asked Elaine.

Mom reached out her hand and stroked Elaine's hair. "Yes, Laney."

Ba drove us home. Mom and Laney sat in the back with me, and Nelson sat up front with Ba. No one fought. We were on the highway for just a minute when Mom and Elaine fell asleep. Happiness, it seemed, could be very tiring.

·CHAPTER·
THREE

IN THE LAST DAYS OF THE BEFORE, BA AND NELSON never stopped fighting. If they were not arguing, it was because one of them was not at home.

"Take it off!" said Ba. We were eating breakfast, and Ba was pointing at the button Nelson was wearing on his shirt. Even though our trip to Williamsport had only been a few days before, that warm feeling had already been stripped away.

Nelson's button showed a hand holding up two fingers for peace. Then it said 1-2-3-4, W.D.W.Y.F.W. Nelson said it basically stood for "We Don't Want Your War" and I could figure out the "F" part for myself. The war in Vietnam had been going on for as long as I could remember; everyone was tired of it.

"Are you saying I can't protest the war?" said Nelson.

"That button is not appropriate," said Ba. Then an idea occurred to him. "Have you been participating in those protests at school?"

Nelson tightened his grip on his fork. "What if I have?"

"The purpose of school is to learn, not to protest," said Ba. "Those protestors have closed down universities, interrupted classes. All of them—and you—should be focused on your studies." I thought Nelson should not be protesting the war for a different reason; last year, the National Guard opened fire on students protesting the war at Kent State. Four of them died.

"That's not the point," said Nelson. "The war in Vietnam is wrong. The United States needs to get out."

Mom gave me a wide-eyed look, one that said, *What are we going to do?* Then she said, "Please, let's not fight."

Ba and Nelson stared at each other, each daring the other to move first.

"Not now," pleaded Mom.

Suddenly, I saw my chance. "Yeah, tomorrow morning would be much better for a fight. Can you argue tomorrow?"

I was taking a chance, being a wise guy, but it worked. Mom smiled, and Ba and Nelson each took a deep breath. I felt like a hero. But then Ba came out of his corner, swinging again.

"You know, when I was your age, I loved jazz. I listened to it all the time. But then my father, your *ye ye,* told me to stop. It was becoming too much," said Ba. He snapped his fingers. "All my records—Charlie Parker, Duke Ellington—*gone*, the next day."

It was hard to imagine my father loving something as wild and unpredictable as jazz. But the point of his story was clear. We were to obey him, no matter what. My father fully believed in the five primary relationships taught by Confucianism: ruler–subject; parent–child; husband–wife; older sibling–younger sibling; friend–friend. Fulfilling these relationships properly, he said, was what kept society running properly. In all the relationships, except friendship, there was someone in charge and someone who was not. Somehow, I always managed to come out on the bottom.

"It's not the same," said Nelson, more to himself than to Ba. "Not the same. We all have an obligation to do what we think is right. To do what we can to make the world a better place."

"A better place," repeated Ba. He snorted slightly into his tea and shook his head.

"Yeah, a better place," said Nelson. He glanced around the room as if looking for an idea. "As a matter of fact, I was thinking that after college, I'll join the Peace Corps."

"Huh. You want to live with starvation and dirty

water? Go back to China," said Ba. We had been to Taiwan once, when I was younger, but none of us kids had ever been to the mainland, not the place my father meant when he said *China* with equal parts bitterness and longing. Still, I wasn't going to be the one to point out that you can't go *back* to a place you've never been. "You're going to get your PhD after you graduate. Or go to medical school."

"We'll see," said Nelson.

"You're not turning into one of those lazy, good-for-nothings I see on the evening news," said Ba. "No job, no skills. They are *not* making the world a better place. Their parents must be dying of shame." While most people use "dying of shame" as an expression, my father made it sound like an actual fatal condition.

Nelson folded his hands together so that his two index fingers stood straight up, like a church steeple, while the rest of his fingers curled tight and low. He pushed the two tall fingers against his lips.

"Take that button off," said Ba, dabbing his mouth on a napkin and getting up from the table. He was getting ready for work. "I have not worked this hard so my son, *my number one son*, can go to another country and sleep on a dirt floor. Do you hear me? Stay away from those protests."

Nelson looked at my father, knowing what he was expected to say, even when it was so clear that he wanted something different. He glanced at me, and then said, "Yes, Ba," as he undid the button and folded it into his hand. His voice twisted, but it did not break.

That afternoon, Nelson began packing to go back to school. I watched him fold his jean jacket and put it in his duffel bag. I wanted a jacket like that. Cool, kind of tough.

I remember thinking Nelson must have been really glad to be going back to school. I wondered what he did with the button.

"So," I said. "Do you really want to join the Peace Corps?" I had never heard him mention that idea before.

Nelson raised one shoulder and let it drop. "Let's say it's a possibility."

"If you don't stay in school, you might get drafted," I said. As long as he stayed in school, Nelson could get a deferment, which meant that he couldn't be drafted to fight in Vietnam.

"But that's not the point. I think the war is wrong, and it's my job to speak up about it, whether or not I have something to gain. It's my duty—and yours—as a member of society."

Nelson talked to me like a grown-up, which I really liked. But I wasn't sure I understood what he was talking about. What society did I belong to? I nodded, like I understood. But I must have still looked confused, because Nelson looked at me and laughed.

"Hey," said Nelson. "Let's get Mom to make us some shrimp chips."

Shrimp chips—that was something I understood.

Shrimp chips are sort of like potato chips—crispy and fried. Ba didn't like them. He said they were too greasy and unhealthy, so we only made them when he was at work. Mom said she would make some, and put oil in a pan to heat up. Then, while we were waiting, she pulled out a booklet with photographs.

"Where'd you find that?" asked Nelson.

"What's that?" I asked at the same time.

"It has pictures of all the incoming freshmen, with their names, hometowns, and stuff," Nelson explained. "It's called a face book. This was the face book for my year."

"Nelson left it out, where anyone could come along and look in it," said Mom, in a singsong voice. In the Before, there were times when Mom was more like us.

"Yeah, well, I won't make that mistake again," said Nelson.

"Is there anyone you like?" asked Mom, holding it slightly out of reach.

Nelson took too long to answer. "Um . . . not really."

"You do! You do!" teased Mom. She picked up the book and flipped through it. "What's her name?"

"Mom . . ."

"Tell me, or I'll just read every girl's name in this book. Alicia Abbott? Catherine Ackerman? Frances Aldridge?" Mom peered at Frances Aldridge, whose thick eyebrows came together in an angry V. "Mmmm . . . I take back that last one. *Not* Frances Aldridge."

"Marjorie Stallings," said Nelson, giving in.

Mom flipped through the book until she reached the S's. She ran her finger down the page. "Oh, Nelson," she said. "She's very pretty. And smart. She looks like a smart girl, don't you think, Peter?"

The girl in the picture had long straight hair that curled up at the end. She was looking up and smiling, like she saw something funny on the ceiling. "She's not completely stupid looking," I offered.

"She actually doesn't live far from here," said Nelson, ignoring my comment. "I'd been meaning to call her, but . . . it might cut into my studying." He tried to sound like he was joking, but I could tell he was still thinking of his argument with Ba.

"You should ask her out," said Mom. "Or do the girls do all the asking these days, with women's liberation?"

"The girls at school, the ones who are into women's lib, you can still ask them out," said Nelson.

"Tell Marjorie that I support the Equal Rights Amendment," said Mom. "I don't see what's so controversial about saying women and men should be treated equally."

"So if the amendment passed, would it be illegal to hold a door open for a woman?" I asked Mom. It would be nice to have that excuse, at least for the more annoying girls at school.

Mom turned to me. "Peter." Mom's voice was soft but stern. "This isn't about manners, and I do expect you to have manners."

"Okay," I said quickly. I hadn't meant for the conversation to get so serious. Usually Ba was the one who turned conversations into lectures about doing well in school or current events. Elaine wandered into the kitchen. She had a book from the library, *A Child's Book of Birds*. "Listen," she said. "What is the only bird that can fly backward?"

Mom squeezed her eyes shut and pretended to think. "A robin?"

"Hummingbirds," said Nelson gently, turning away from the window and tapping Elaine on the nose.

"Hummingbirds fly backward. They can also fly sideways and even upside-down."

Elaine turned the page. "Cor-rect!"

For one disloyal moment, I thought about what it would be like without Ba, just the four of us. We wouldn't fight. I wouldn't get extra homework. We would make jokes and eat shrimp chips.

Then I pushed the thought away.

"I want to see a hummingbird," said Elaine. "I don't care what kind. I don't have any on my life list." Elaine kept a list of all the birds she had ever seen.

"You will," said Nelson. "When you're older, you'll travel and see lots of birds. You're so smart to start when you're young. You'll have a huge life list when you grow up."

Mom leaned over the stove, checking the wok filled partway with oil. She put the handle of a wooden spoon in the pan of oil and checked for bubbles.

Mom opened the box of shrimp chips and poured some in her hand. They were hard, glassy little pieces, but once they hit the oil, they bubbled and bloomed. Mom carefully spooned them onto a paper towel and motioned for us to take one.

"You first, Mom," said Nelson. Mom picked up one of them and ate it, closing her eyes.

I took one, too. I liked to let it rest on my tongue so I could feel the little bubbles pop and stick to my tongue.

"Any girl who goes out with you is a lucky girl," said Mom, looking at Nelson. Nelson had gotten taller than Mom, so she had to look up a little. "Call her," Mom urged. "Your father hasn't forgotten what it's like to be a young man."

"Yeah, yeah," said Nelson, blushing a little. And then Mom laughed again. Mom had been born in China, but she had come to the United States when she was a baby. I had always thought that was why she laughed more easily than Ba, who did not come to the States until he had finished college.

I have this picture in my head of my mom in the kitchen, tilting her head up as she laughed. Ba always said he wanted to marry her the minute he heard her laugh, and for a moment, I understood why Nelson wanted to talk to girls.

Nelson called Marjorie, and they ended up making plans to go out to a movie after dinner. Meanwhile, my best friend, Chris, stopped by and said he wanted to get a game together at Folger's Lot. We didn't actually know anyone named Folger, but that's what we'd called the lot for as long as I could remember, and Nelson before me.

"Sounds good to me," I said, grabbing my glove. Me and Chris, we would play baseball every day of the summer if you let us.

"Hey, Nelson, you should come with us," said Chris. He tried to say it like he didn't care, but we all knew that if Nelson came and played, we'd beat just about anyone.

"Well . . ." Nelson scratched his head. "I've got this date . . ."

"Oh, he doesn't want to get all messed up for his date with a *girl*," I said.

Chris joined in. "Oh, no kisses for sweaty, dirty Nelson," he sang in a high voice. He made loud smacking noises. We laughed like crazy.

Nelson picked up a pen and threw it at me. "All right, all right. Just for a little bit."

"Can I come, too?" begged Laney. She always wanted to stick her nose in where it didn't belong.

"No," I told her. "There won't be any girls there."

When the other kids heard that Nelson was coming to play, even for just a little bit, they all came down to the lot. Nelson brought his lucky bat, a Louisville Slugger with red tape on the handle. He'd hit fifty-two home runs with that bat. Out-of-the-park home runs at the school where the fields were fenced in. Lost-in-the-woods home runs here at the lot. Barn burners at the plate, catcher versus runner. He'd notched them all on that bat.

We had enough kids that we could play full sided, instead of calling right field out or having ghost runners. It was a really beautiful night—it wasn't your typical end-of-summer night, when it's so hot the air shimmers over the road. A tiny cool breeze fanned us in the outfield. While we waited for our turn at bat, we watched the clouds glow purple and blue, edged in orange.

When it was time for Nelson's at bat, we let the other team have an extra outfielder. They also put up their best pitcher, Nick, who was a lefty and had had an early growth spurt to boot. Nelson fouled off the first pitch. The next pitch was way on the outside.

Donny Sherman, who was playing catcher, called a strike.

Nelson looked at Donny. "You must be joking."

"I call 'em like I see 'em," responded Donny.

He was 0–2, but Nelson didn't look nervous. Nick went into his windup, and the next thing I heard was a dull pop. The ball sailed out past the outfield and into the trees. A shooting star.

For a second, everyone was quiet, just watching the ball soar away from the field. Then everyone began whooping and cheering. Nelson trotted around the bases, trying not to look too pleased with himself. When he reached home, Donny took off his mask and shook Nelson's hand.

Nelson picked up his bat, jogged over to our side, and handed it to me. "Gotta go. Can't keep a girl waiting."

"Come on, Nelson, just a little longer," I said. "It's not even hot. You're not getting sweaty." How could a girl even compare to a decent ball game? Girls couldn't even play ball, as far as I could tell. A cool breeze fanned the field. It looked like it might rain. I didn't want to lose that feeling, like everything I could ever want was right here. Not yet.

Nelson laughed and shook his head. "I'll stay home tomorrow night, play a whole game with you guys. Maybe we can even work on that palmball," he promised. When I scowled at him, he said, "One day you'll understand."

When I think about this moment, I wonder what would have happened if I had tried harder to get him to stay, for just a little longer. One more at bat, one more inning, one more anything. If I had just changed my grip ever so slightly, and let things spin differently. Instead, I went on playing, believing him.

• • •

This is the last moment I remember in the Before: seeing red and blue lights reflecting on my walls late that night. The lights woke me up, and for a moment I just lay in bed, half-awake, thinking they looked kind of pretty in the dark.

Red.
Blue.
Red.
Blue.

My brain didn't process any more than that, not until I heard something that sounded like an animal caught in a trap, a sound that wasn't human. It started as a high-pitched squeal and slowly opened to a full-throated, raw howl.

I didn't see it coming. I went down looking.

• CHAPTER •
FOUR

THEY TELL US HE DIDN'T SUFFER. NELSON DIED INSTANTLY.
Meadowbrook Road had gotten slick from the rain when
Nelson lost control of the car and hit a tree. One police
officer said that maybe Nelson had swerved to avoid hitting an animal that had darted into the road.

My father clenched his fists when he heard that. His
knuckles turned white and the veins in his hands bulged.
"I always told Nelson, the life of a person is more important than the life of an animal," he said.

I wonder if Nelson thought about that—that he was
disobeying Ba.

I hope what they said is true about the suffering, that
he did not suffer at all. Maybe Nelson was changing sta-
tions on the radio, or thinking about that girl, Marjorie
Stallings, since he had just dropped her off. Sometimes
when I can't sleep, I think maybe we are suffering more
because Nelson didn't suffer at all, and there's just a certain amount of pain that has to be endured. I'm okay

with that. I'm okay with carrying that for Nelson, though I wonder if we will ever be done.

Sometimes I have this dream that I'm in the car with Nelson, and on the way home, I say, "Hey, Nelson, you should slow down here." And Nelson says okay, and we drive all the way down Meadowbrook Road with no problem. But I always wake up before we make it home, and then I have to lie in bed, not moving, while my brain tells the rest of me that it's only a dream.

•CHAPTER•
FIVE

IN BASEBALL, THERE ARE THE RULES THAT EVERYONE knows, and the rules that you have to figure out for yourself. For example, the first rule every kid learns in baseball is it's three strikes and you're out. Then there are rules you have to figure out—like if you strike out, you don't cry on your way back to the dugout, even if you just got the third out and your team's behind. You hold your head high, walk like a man, and act like you're gonna hit it out of the park on your next turn. If you don't, you'll get picked last for the next game.

There are rules when people die, too. Some of them everyone knows, and some you have to figure out for yourself.

On the morning of Nelson's funeral, I remember waking up and finding Liao *Ai Yi* holding my shirt.

It was strange to see Auntie Liao in my bedroom; she usually stayed in the kitchen with Mom. She held up a small black fabric rectangle, about three inches long and an inch high, and two tiny safety pins.

"Normally you wear a black armband for mourning. But when I talked to your father, he was concerned that people would think you were protesting the war. So, we decided you should wear something on your shirt." She pinned the black fabric to my shirt pocket.

"You wear it every day," said Auntie Liao. "And you must not wear red. Red is the Chinese color for happiness, you know? You wear only dark colors, and no red."

I never wanted to wear red again.

We were getting ready to go to the funeral when the phone rang. We were in the front hall, dark suits and dresses. Mom and Elaine each pinned a white scrap of cloth in their hair. We had our shoes on—we were that close to leaving. Ba answered the phone.

I could tell from the way he spoke in an extra-loud voice that it was a call from Taiwan. That, and the fact that it was a short call because calls from overseas are very expensive.

After he hung up, Ba came to talk to Laney and me. "Nai Nai says that you should not go to the funeral."

"What?" I said. "Why not?" I hardly knew Nai Nai, my father's mother. We had gone to Taiwan only once, when I was five. I remembered she had goldfish in her garden pond and she would let me feed them stale bread.

Ba didn't answer right away. "It's okay—I didn't want to go," said Laney quietly.

"Well, I do." I wanted to explain some more, but none of my thoughts could be formed into words.

"Nai Nai believes that, as children, you are risking exposure to bad spirits," Ba explained. "Your souls are unformed." He rubbed his face, pulling his fingers across his cheeks. "It is not an uncommon belief."

Bad spirits? Unformed souls? My father, man of science, never spoke that way. "Do you believe in this, Ba?"

"Your Nai Nai has made this request, and we must honor it," said Ba, not answering my question.

"She's in *Taiwan*. She doesn't have to know anything."

Ba grabbed my arm, surprising me. His fingers felt like they were pressing right into the bone. "We are not supposed to have a funeral at all," he said in a sharp, low voice. "No black bands. Do you understand? This is not supposed to happen; white hair is attending the funeral of the black hair. *This is not supposed to happen.*" He pulled me closer to him. I stared at the frown lines around his mouth. I wasn't sure what he meant: that Nelson wasn't supposed to die or we weren't supposed to have the funeral.

I jerked my arm away from him. "No one in this house has white hair. You're punishing me, for something I didn't do," I said.

"It isn't a punishment. You may not like what Nai Nai is asking you to do, but this is how you show respect."

I turned to Mom, who had starting washing dishes. She was down to one plate, which she washed over and over. "Mom, you think Laney and I should go, don't you?"

Mom didn't look at me. She stared out the window, the one over the sink. "Do as your father says, Peter."

Mom had been my last hope. Laney and I didn't go.

There is a button on our TV, one you have to adjust so that all the separate little black and white dots come together, tinier and tinier, until the picture comes into focus. I didn't know then that my mom had become like those tiny dots, far apart, out of the picture.

· CHAPTER · SIX

MOM STOPPED COOKING NEXT. THE FIRST TIME IT happened, Ba came home from work and was surprised not to find dinner on the table. You could tell he was surprised, because he stood in the middle of the kitchen, opening and closing his mouth, and looking around.

Elaine and I were not surprised, though, because we had watched Mom watch TV all afternoon. She did not move, not even to adjust the picture when it got fuzzy.

"Your mother did not cook dinner?" he asked. "I told her the casseroles were all gone."

"No," Elaine and I told him. "There's no dinner."

Ba picked up his keys and began putting his shoes back on. "Your mother must not be feeling well," he told us. "I will go pick up some dinner. I will be right back. Don't bother your mother."

Ba came back with a big brown paper bag. By this time, Elaine and I were very hungry, and Elaine began calling out the different dishes as she unhooked the top of each carton. I set the table while Ba changed out of his work clothes.

"Cashew chicken," she said. "Shrimp fried rice. Moo shu pork."

Without even thinking, I said, "That's Nelson's favorite." Because it was.

As soon as I said it, Elaine tilted her head toward the doorway. Mom was standing there, watching us. And then she was gone.

That's Nelson's favorite.

Suddenly his name seemed odd and foreign, a stranger among us. I tried to recall the last time I heard his name, and I couldn't. Where did it go?

His name had trickled away slowly, so slowly I hadn't even noticed. I tried to retrace my steps. Somewhere along the way, he had gone from Nelson to "your brother" to "your loss" to nothing, a name with no place among us. I remember when people said "your loss." It sounded like we had lost an umbrella or a set of keys—something replaceable.

All through dinner that night, the food felt hard and dry in my throat. Mom had been eating with us less and less. This time, though, it was my fault. She had been in the doorway, and I had scared her off, like one of Laney's birds.

At that moment, I understood I was not supposed to say Nelson's name anymore. That was a rule I had to learn for myself.

After Ba brought home Chinese takeout, Mom didn't cook again. She stopped leaving the house and pretty much started staying on the couch in the living room, like an island in a carpeted sea. Sometimes she watches TV all afternoon until late at night. Sometimes she doesn't do anything at all except sit.

She has really only gotten up once, as far as I know, which was to pack up all of Nelson's stuff. His room just became empty one day, without so much as a speck of dust left behind.

Maybe Mom is following rules, too.

The problem with rules is that they're not meant to change anything. Rules are meant to keep order, like writing your name at the top of the page.

If nothing changes soon, I think I'll go crazy.

• CHAPTER •
SEVEN

THERE ARE TWENTY-FIVE STUDENTS IN MS. ROWE'S history class. I know this because when she asks us to choose partners for a unit on presidential elections, twelve pairs of students immediately form. Twelve pairs, and me.

Here's another rule nobody tells you. If something bad happens to you, you better start acting normal pretty quickly, or your friends will start leaving you alone. If you don't act sufficiently excited when the Pirates win the World Series, for example, you are in trouble.

Chris pairs up with Tom Faitz. During the play-offs, Tom refused to change his socks until the Pirates won the pennant, and then kept wearing the same socks through the World Series. I guess he and Chris bonded over that. Chris will want to do something about FDR because he's a nut about World War II. I wonder if Tom knows that.

Ms. Rowe puts her hand on my shoulder. "Peter," she says brightly. "Shall we add you to another group? You all could study one of the great three-party elections.

The election of 1912 had Republicans, Democrats, and Teddy Roosevelt's Bull Moose party."

"It's okay," I say. "I don't mind working alone."

This answer does not please Ms. Rowe. "I know! *I* can be your partner."

I know that Ms. Rowe means well, she really does. She's one of the youngest teachers in the school, and she wears her hair long and straight, like the students, instead of hair-sprayed and in a bun, like the other teachers. She's one of those teachers who always wants to know how you're feeling and gives you points for sharing. What she doesn't realize, though, is that she's making things worse.

"No," I say. Then I add, "Thank you."

"You'll have to do two reports, one about the winning candidate, and one about the losing candidate," she warns me.

Now Chris and Tom have taken Melissa Albrecht's notebook and are pretending to read through it. Melissa squeals and reaches for it, but she doesn't really seem to mind.

"I'll do both," I tell Ms. Rowe. "It's not a big deal."

The bell rings and everyone starts gathering up their books, but Ms. Rowe does not leave my desk.

Ms. Rowe kneels down next to me. "Peter," she says. "I think you and I know that there's something else going on here, yes?" She puts her hand on top of mine. "Is there anything you'd like to talk about? About your family, perhaps?"

I quickly pull my hand out from under hers, and then check to make sure no one saw, especially Chris. "No!" I say. "Everything is fine."

"Really?" she says, poking out her lower lip. "I know *I* always feel better when I can rap with a friend about my problems."

"I don't have any friends," I say, closing my textbook with a snap. My ears turn hot when I hear my own mistake. "I mean, I don't have any *problems*."

My chat with Ms. Rowe makes me late for English with Miss Gunderson. When I hand Miss Gunderson my late pass, she pulls her glasses to the end of her nose and sniffs, like a watchdog smelling a stranger.

"I see you were with Ms. Rowe," she says, dragging out the *zzzz* sound of *Ms.*

"Yes, ma'am," I say, trying to get back under the radar as soon as possible.

Miss Gunderson is definitely a hair-spray-and-bun teacher. She is not interested in being my friend, or anyone else's friend, for that matter. "I don't understand these young people, trying to introduce some new form of address, when *Miss* and *Mrs.* have been doing perfectly well for centuries. It's nonsense if you ask me."

Ms. Rowe is the first teacher at my school to use *Ms.*, which, as far as I could figure, was meant to blend *Miss* and *Mrs.* What no one has been able to explain to me, though, is what *Ms.* is short for.

When I don't respond, Miss Gunderson continues, "I suppose I should just be thankful that she's not asking you to call her by her Christian name. I understand *that's* becoming quite popular in the more liberal enclaves."

Ms. Rowe's note puts Miss Gunderson in such a bad mood that she announces that we have a pop quiz. "We do things the old-fashioned way in this room," she announces. She claps her hands together for emphasis. "The! Old! Fashioned! Way!"

For once, I'm on Miss Gunderson's side, even though everyone around me grumbles as they take out clean sheets of paper to answer questions about Steinbeck's *The Pearl*. It's not that I'm going to do well—I've only read the first ten pages and I barely remember what happened. It's just that I'll take cruelty over pity any day.

As soon as the school doors open, I run. I spin past the clumps of little kids and moms, the bigger kids, and the buses. I let the houses and mailboxes go by in a blur, listening to my feet slap along the sidewalk. *Thwack thwack thwack.* I leap over the curbs and listen to the dogs bark. I run until the air begins to burn my lungs, and my legs beg to stop.

I run every day after school. It's easier than trying to figure out who will—or more likely, will not—walk with me.

I check my watch; it is 3:26. Not bad. I sit on the concrete front steps of the house, breathing hard.

"Here he is," says a voice. "The most loyal customer of the United States Postal Service."

I shade my eyes and look up. "Hi, Mr. Kerns." Mr. Kerns is our mailman.

He hands me a thin bundle of mail. "There you go, Peter. Still not trusting that mailbox, huh?" Mr. Kerns's eyes crinkle up at his own joke.

If you had told me in the Before that one day my life would revolve around Mr. Kerns, the mailman, I might have laughed at you.

Instead, though, I go into the house and sort the mail on the counter. There is a bill from the water company, which I put to the side for Ba. For Mom, though, there is a new issue of *Family Circle* magazine. One of the headlines promises recipes for quick and easy meals. Perfect.

I roll the magazine into my hand and walk into the living room.

"Hi, Mom. I'm home." I try to make my voice bright against the darkness.

I wait for Mom to answer. Sometimes she does, but you have to give her a few moments.

"Hi," says Mom. She has a blanket draped across her shoulders and is watching *Days of Our Lives*.

"Look, Mom." I unfurl the magazine. "You have a new issue of *Family Circle*."

Mom looks at the magazine in my hand, but does not try to take it. "Maybe I'll look at it later."

I give the magazine a little shake. "There's recipes in here. Easy ones." I hold it a little closer to her. "Here."

"Not now, Peter," says Mom. She does not even try to take it. "Please." She pushes deeper under the blanket, and stares at the television. She is getting very thin; even with the blanket over her, you can tell that there is not much there.

After I had messed up about Nelson's name, I started to think about all the other ways that Nelson's name might come into the house. I decided my job was to protect my mom from letters addressed to Nelson, from stupid people and machines that don't know not to send him mail anymore. That's why I have to be home every day after school, to get the mail. I've intercepted letters from the Harmony Record & Tape Club (*Twelve records for only a penny, Mr. Lee!*), a postcard from a girl named Natalie, and a couple of magazines. Each time, I tear them up and take the pieces out to the garbage can.

Sorting the mail is a lot trickier than it sounds, because it's not just about keeping things out, it's what I let in. Back during Christmas, for instance, it was really tough. Stupidly cheerful cards—dancing snowmen, crazy Santas—out. Quiet cards with candles or wreaths, and sayings like "Season's Greetings"—in. The hardest ones were pictures of families. Whole, smiling families. They made me wonder if we ever took a picture, if people would be able to see what was missing.

It's all kind of stupid, I know, sorting mail and presenting magazines like I wrote them myself, but it's the only thing I know how to do.

Nelson used to say that the great athletes are great because they're consistent—anyone can have a flash of brilliance, but the really good ones show up day after day and perform. Lou Gehrig played with broken bones; he even stayed in the game after getting hit in the head. So bringing in the mail every day—that's what I do. It's the only thing I can think of.

·CHAPTER·
EIGHT

I THINK I HAVE HAD A PRETTY BAD DAY AT SCHOOL until Elaine comes home.

"Hey, Laney," I say.

Elaine shoves her way past me.

"Leave me alone!" she screams. Then she punches me in the arm before she runs up to her room.

If Elaine had done something like this in the Before, I'm pretty sure Mom would have gone after her and found out what's wrong. Then again, Elaine didn't do things like this in the Before.

I listen for a moment, hoping that I'll hear Mom get up and move. Nothing.

I walk up to Elaine's room and knock on the door frame. Elaine is sitting on her bed, with her eyes wide open and the bottom of her face squeezed up. Her nostrils are flaring. I know that trick. You make that face when you don't want to cry.

"Um." I'm not sure what to say. "Everything okay, Laney?"

Elaine blinks hard and the not-crying face goes away. "No, everything is *not* okay." She swipes her nose with her shoulder.

I take a step back, out of punching range. "What's the matter?"

"We're supposed to bring something for the bake sale tomorrow," says Elaine. "We're raising money for our class field trip to the zoo."

I don't understand why this is a crisis. Laney loves the zoo, the bird house most of all.

"So, do you want to call Ba and ask him to bring home cookies from the store?" We're not really supposed to call Ba at work unless it's an emergency, but from the way Elaine is acting, I can say it is one.

"No," says Elaine. "That's the problem. It can't be store-bought. My teacher said so. It's supposed to be *home-made*." Her face turns bright red and she looks like she's really going to cry. "'Please make sure your mothers make something special,'" she says, in a voice that is supposed to her teacher's.

I wish she would go back to being mad; it's easier than her crying. Mom used to make all of this stuff—the cupcakes, the cookies with sprinkles. Lemon chiffon cake.

"It's not the end of the world," I say, though, clearly, Elaine thinks it is.

"*Everybody* is going to bring something. *Everybody* but me is going to raise money for the field trip. And then everyone's going to say, 'Ohhhh, look at Elaine—she didn't have anything for the bake sale.'"

I wish I had something to say, something wise and big-brotherly that would make her perk up and smile.

"Sorry, Laney." I turn to go. "Wish I could help."

"Wait," says Elaine. She makes a hiccuping sound. "Can *you* make something?"

"Me? Boys don't cook." At school, only girls take home ec, which is sewing and cooking and stuff. Boys take shop.

"Daddy cooks."

"That's like eggs and stuff; you're asking me to *bake*. Baking is different." Even as I say the words, I realize they don't really make sense. Cooking, baking—it's all about making food. It's just that Mom is supposed to be doing the baking.

Elaine crosses her arms and lets out a huge sigh. I think about Elaine in Williamsport, skipping around with the two flags, trying to make the game so that she'd be happy either way. It's not fair.

"How about I help you turn on the oven and stuff, but you do the main baking part?" I ask Laney.

You'd think I'd given her a million dollars. She jumps up and hugs me. "You're the best, Peter! The best, best, best!"

"It's not that big a deal," I say. "I'm just turning on the oven."

Of course, I end up having to help Elaine a lot more than just turning on the oven. I help her find a box of chocolate cake mix in the pantry, and take out the oil and eggs. When Elaine explodes an egg into the batter, I convince her that kids like chocolate cupcakes with a surprise crunch. And after she says her arm is getting tired in the middle of mixing the batter, I have to do some of the mixing, too.

While the cupcakes are in the oven, Sean Tyrell knocks on the back door of the kitchen. He lives behind us and goes to St. Leo's, the Catholic school, instead of public school. He's not exactly my friend, but then again, he's the only one who comes over now.

"Wanna go play ball?" asks Sean. "They're getting a game together over at the lot."

"He can't!" chirps Elaine before I have a chance to say anything. "Peter is helping *me* make cupcakes."

I can see from Sean's expression that I might as well

be wearing a frilly apron and twirling around the kitchen like Julia Child.

"She needed them for school," I mumble. "I just turned on the oven, mostly."

Sean nods slowly. The oven timer dings. "Do you want a cupcake?" offers Elaine. "They're chocolate." Sean smiles and starts to take a seat at the table.

"I won't even charge you the full price," adds Elaine.

"Charge me?" Sean looks startled.

"This is for *education*," says Elaine with great dignity. "I'm going to charge a quarter a piece at school. I'm going to the bird house at the zoo to see the kingfisher and a tanager." She rips off a piece of waxed paper and lines the bottom of a shoe box I found for her, making neat little folded corners. Mom taught her that.

"Tell you what," says Sean. "Let me try a bite for free, and if I like it, I'll give you a dime."

"What if you *don't* like it?" asks Elaine. She puts her hands on top of the box.

"If *I* don't like it, then you probably shouldn't be selling them," says Sean. He has a point. Sean has what some people might call a *healthy appetite*. Even though he and I are close to the same height, Sean probably outweighs me by a good twenty or thirty pounds.

Elaine reluctantly hands over one cupcake, and Sean makes a big deal out of sniffing the cupcake first, and then taking a small bite and chewing it very precisely. Then he swallows, digs into his pocket, and pulls out a dime.

"Yay!" says Elaine. She does a funny little dance. Now she reminds me of the old Elaine. "They're good! Peter, do you want one for helping me?"

"Sure," I say. Elaine gives me a cupcake, and then carefully drops Sean's dime into her shirt pocket.

When I watch her pocket the money, though, I realize that something is missing.

"You're not wearing your black band," I say. The words come out before my brain can even process them.

Her hand flies up and touches the spot where the strip is supposed to go. I can tell that she isn't even looking for it; she already knows it isn't there. She's trying to cover up the spot.

Elaine mumbles something.

"What did you say?"

"Ba said we could take it off." She says the words so softly they seem to float out of her mouth.

"He said *could*. That doesn't mean *have to*." That day, when Ba said we didn't have to wear the black bands anymore, I had looked at Elaine, and she had looked at me, and neither one of us had moved to take them off. I thought we had understood each other.

Sean is eating his cupcake without looking at either one of us. I wonder how crazy I sound. I can hear a TV commercial coming from the living room; Mom can probably hear us, too. Ba always tells us to be careful of the face we show to the world, that family things stayed within the family. Now I know why he says those things, but I can't stop myself.

"So, you just stopped wearing it? Just like that?" My words snap in the air, even as I lower my voice.

"Peter," Elaine pleads. "Don't be mad."

I push back my chair from the table. "You know what? Do whatever you want. I was done helping you, anyway."

I walk out into the backyard and try to act like I know what I am doing out here. I grab a branch that has fallen in the yard and take a couple of swings with it, pretending to clobber some unseen ball heading my way.

"She's just a kid," says Sean, who has followed me outside.

"She still should have . . ." I say. I swing the branch harder and search for the right words. "I mean, she should have known." I'm not making any sense; I'm not sure what Elaine should have known.

"When I was younger, I used to take off my scapular when no one was looking because it itched me." Sean reaches into his shirt and pulls out something that looks like two tags on a long piece of elastic. "I wasn't thinking about what I was supposed to be doing, about God or anything. I just wanted to be comfortable. Maybe it's something like that?"

"The band wasn't next to her skin," I say. Still, I appreciate that Sean is trying to help.

Swinging the branch feels good. If I swing fast enough, I can hear a little zinging noise as the little branches cut through the air.

"So, you want to go over and play some ball?" Sean pantomimes a throw. "The guys want to get in some practice before tryouts."

Now here is the truth. I had been a little relieved when Elaine said I couldn't go. The thought of playing baseball, even just sandlot ball, scares me a little. It is too close to Nelson, too close without him being there. But this isn't anything I can explain to anyone.

At the same time, though, I miss it. It doesn't seem like spring without baseball. The ball fields look so pretty when the grass comes out. I remember how good it feels to stand with the other kids and chant to the batter, urging him on:

G-double-o-D E-Y-E, good eye! Good eye!

Way to watch! Way to watch!

Way to watch that ball go by!

It is all so dazzling and loud. It's like looking at the sun, though—if you look too long, your eyes hurt.

"I don't know," I say. "Probably not."

"You know, some of the other guys are saying . . ." Sean stops.

"What?"

"I dunno. You don't like baseball anymore."

"Let me guess who said this. Chris." Chris goes to church with Sean. He used to joke about Sean and how much he ate, but now he probably jokes about me.

"They didn't say it in a mean way. Chris was just saying you're not playing ball at recess or anything." Some of the guys bring their gloves and bats to school so we can play at recess. That was something I did last year.

I take the branch and crack it over my knee, snapping it in two. It kind of hurts and feels good at the same time. "I don't care."

"I'll probably go to tryouts." Sean rubs the back of his neck. "My old man really wants me to play, on a team, I mean."

"Well." It's so easy for him to talk about playing ball. A pang of jealousy makes my chest ache. "Good luck."

"You should come," says Sean. "We could try out together."

The harder Sean tries to convince me, the louder the no gets in my head.

"I don't know. I think I've outgrown that now," I say, sticking my chin out a little. "It's kind of for babies."

It really kills me to say that.

Sean puts his hands in his pockets. "Okay, yeah, see you." He turns to go.

I wonder if Sean will come back, or if he will be like the others.

•CHAPTER•
NINE

A FEW DAYS LATER, WHILE I AM CHECKING THE MAIL, I find a letter to Mr. and Mrs. Chen Lee, the parents of Peter Lee. It is from my school. They must have gotten Ba's name from the school records because most people call him John.

If teachers at school want to send a note home, they just hand it to the kid in a plain white envelope. If it is something official from the school, it has to be bad. Your-kid-is-failing bad.

I saw this TV show where the guy needed to open a letter without anyone knowing that he had done it. He held the envelope over a steaming kettle until the steam had warmed up the glue on the envelope and the flap popped open.

What they *didn't* show on TV was that the water makes the envelope all wrinkly. I hope that Ba will not notice.

Dear Mr. and Mrs. Lee,

*I am Melanie Rowe, Peter's social studies
teacher. With the permission of our principal,
Mrs. Wright, I am starting an after-school
peer group for students who need a secure,
confidential environment to discuss any issue
that is troubling them. I would like to
recommend Peter for this group. There is no
charge for this service, and I think Peter might
benefit. Please contact me to discuss this further.*

> *Sincerely,*
> *Melanie Rowe*
> *Highcliff Junior High*

I read the letter a couple of times and then put it on the counter, resisting the urge to crumple it. Why can't *Ms.* Rowe just leave me alone? I don't need to talk to *anyone* in a "secure, confidential environment." That's for people like Ginnie Clark, who cries a lot, and Kenny Higgins, who always, *always* gets picked last in gym.

I look at the rest of the mail. There is a newspaper bill and a postcard from the dentist, reminding us it is time for a six-month checkup. I set the bill to the side and pick up the postcard, which has a picture of a smiling dentist on the front. The postcard will have to do. I leave the letter on the counter.

"Look, Mom," I say, bringing her the postcard. "A note from the dentist."

"Mmm hmmm."

I try harder. "You need to make an appointment, for me and Elaine."

Mom picks up the postcard, glances at it, and sets it down. "Maybe later."

In the Before, Mom would pick us up from school early, and take us out to lunch before our appointments. She said she felt so lucky to have healthy children. Three healthy children.

I stand there, trying to think of something else to say, when I hear the sound of a key in the lock. *Ba is home early!*

I run into the kitchen, and add some cold water to the kettle so it will stop steaming. Elaine walks in. "What are you doing?"

"None of your business." This is actually the first conversation we've had since we made cupcakes.

I hear the door open and close, and then the sound of Ba groaning slightly while he takes off his shoes. I pick up the letter and the envelope, hesitating.

"What is that?' asks Elaine.

I shake my head slightly, fold the paper in thirds, and stick it in my back pocket. I've decided: No one is going to find out about the letter.

"Shhh." I put my fingers to my lips.

Elaine looks at me, her mouth slightly open. Then Ba walks in.

Elaine is staring at my back pocket. All she has to do is say, "Peter has something in his pocket," and I am in deep, deep trouble. And she just might, after the business I gave her about the black band.

"What are you doing in here? I hope you are not spoiling your dinner," says Ba.

"I just wanted Peter . . ." begins Elaine.

Oh no. Here goes. I am dead meat.

". . . to get me a glass of milk." Elaine points at the cupboard. "The glass with the pink flowers, okay?" Her face is pure innocence.

I lean slightly so that the counter can hold me up.

"Peter, please get drinks for everyone," says Ba. "I would like water."

I watch Elaine carefully all through dinner. She eats and talks and drinks, the same way she always has. You never would have guessed she saved me.

That night, I go to her room. She is reading in bed—
Little House on the Prairie.

"Thanks, Laney," I say, standing in her doorway.

Elaine looks up. "For what?"

"You know," I make a circle in the air with my hand. "Not saying anything about that paper."

She flips the book over, keeping it open so she won't lose her place. "Are you in trouble?"

"It's nothing. It's a letter from school, but it's not about grades or anything, okay?" I don't want her to change her mind about not telling.

"Okay." Then she says, "And you don't say anything about the band anymore."

"Is that why you did it?" I check behind me, to make sure Ba can't hear us.

"No, I just didn't want you to get into trouble with Ba." Elaine runs her finger over the cover. Two little girls stare at her from the back of a covered wagon. "But I don't want you to be mad at me anymore, either."

I walk into the room and kneel down, so that my chest is the same level as the bed. Laney is wearing a light-blue nightgown. I spread my arms across the top of the bed.

"How did you decide? I mean, to stop wearing it?"

Elaine thinks a minute. "I don't know. One day, it just didn't feel right."

I haven't changed into my pajamas yet; I am still in the clothes I wore to school. I reach up and feel the band between my fingers. It is hard to explain, but in a way, wearing this tiny strip of cloth makes me feel protected, safe, like I have a a shield against the world.

•CHAPTER•
TEN

MAIL FROM TAIWAN COMES ON SPECIAL THIN BLUE airmail paper, a single sheet, with dotted lines and gummed flaps so that when you fold it up, the letter becomes an envelope, too. The letters from Taiwan always have the addresses written out so precisely, with the same careful strokes as the Chinese characters. I wonder if the senders actually know what they are writing, or if they are just copying the shapes.

I hand the letter to Mom, while holding the weekly town newspaper that also came in the mail. In the Before, Mom loved getting the light-blue letters. She would read them over and over, laughing at some parts, running her finger over parts she wanted to read more carefully.

This time she carefully splits the flaps with a hairpin, but after looking at the letter for a minute, she sets it down. "I'll look at it later," she says, as if the effort of holding up the delicate blue paper is too much.

"Who is it from?" I ask.

"My cousin. You never met her." I can feel her folding up, moving away from me. We are in the same room, but she is somewhere else.

I want to have a conversation about something, *anything*. I am playing a one-sided game of catch—I keep throwing the ball, but nothing comes back. I don't know how long I can keep going. But I have to.

"Is everything okay? In the letter I mean?"

"It's fine, Peter," said Mom.

It's *fine*? What she says is so obviously wrong, so obviously not what is happening, that something snaps inside me. I slap the newspaper on the table.

Mom looks at me, surprised. Instantly, I am ashamed and try to cover up.

"I, uh, just wish that I could read some Chinese," I lie. I point to some characters on the airmail envelope. "What does this say? Does it say China?"

My question works, pulling her back. "Look," she says. She smooths the envelope with her fingers. When I reach out to touch the envelope I see that my fingers are almost as long as hers. "That character means 'middle,' and the one next to it means 'country.'" She pauses, and then points to a different part of the envelope. "The whole line says, 'Taiwan, Republic of China.'"

It is almost too much to hope for: a conversation, a

tiny bit more coming back than what I offered. I swallow hard and try to think quickly.

"What about this?" I say, pointing to the stamp on the envelope. The stamp is a picture of a boy at bat. "What does that say? On the bottom?"

Mom actually brings the envelope closer to her face to examine it. "It's for the Little League World Series."

My heart stops. I don't know what to say. Am I allowed to talk about the Before? "Like Williamsport?"

Mom reaches over and brushes my hair lightly. My scalp tingles. "That was a good day, wasn't it, Peter?"

I nod, afraid to speak. If I say the wrong thing, the conversation could end. But I have to say something.

"I remember the guy at the game, the one who gave out all the flags," I say, picking something safe.

"Elaine wanted one of each flag, an American flag and a flag for Taiwan, so that she would be fair," says Mom.

"Twenty-two strikeouts for Taiwan," I say. "A record." *Bie huang. Bie ji. Jiu hao hao tou qiu.* Don't be scared. Don't be nervous. Keep pitching.

Mom looks at me, and then, she smiles.

She smiles.

It is one of those things you are afraid to take your eyes off of, like a bird that flutters onto the arm of your chair. Part of me wants to run, get Elaine to see, and part of me doesn't dare move.

Please stay this way.

I will sit here and look at this postage stamp with you forever if you let things stay this way.

"It was a good day," Mom says softly. "For all of us." All of us.

"I like baseball," I say. It's stupid. But I can't think of what else to say and stay within the rules. I wish she would touch my hair again.

"You do," says Mom. She pauses. "You *love* baseball." She looks at me, as if she is just remembering.

This is better than any birthday or Christmas present I've ever gotten. It makes me bold. "I wish," I start to say. "I wish."

In the Before, Mom would lean closer and say, "What? What do you wish for? Tell me." But in the After, it is too much to expect, even in this moment. I lose my concentration, and I can't think of the right words to say. And as quickly as it came, the moment is gone. Mom curls up on the couch, under her blanket, away from me.

I scramble for a way to bring her back. I pick up the envelope and point to a second, smaller stamp. "Tell me what this stamp says," I say.

No answer.

"Remember the cake you made when we went to the Series? The lemon chiffon?"

While I wait for her to answer, I realize my hands are clenched into fists. I force myself to uncurl them and take a breath.

"I'm tired, Peter." That's my cue to leave. *Don't bother your mother.*

I walk out of the room and head upstairs to my room, my mind swirling with questions. What was different this time? What got her to talk? The fact that it was a Wednesday? The weather? How am I going to make this happen again? I look down at my clothes, searching for something different.

Nelson's room is the first one at the top of the stairs. The door is closed, plain. Nelson had a Roberto Clemente poster on his door, one he got from a pack of baseball cards. I remember liking coming up the stairs and seeing his smiling face at the top.

Then it hits me.

Oceans of green grass and clean white baseballs and thousands of people cheering. The Howard J. Lamade Stadium and flags for Taiwan and the United States.

Fireflies.

I know what I have to do.

· CHAPTER ·
ELEVEN

"YOU WANT TO PLAY BASEBALL?" ASKS MY FATHER. "NOW?"

I put down my fork and try to figure out the best way to say yes. I spent a long time that afternoon thinking about how to get my father to let me play baseball. I decided to start out by making dinner. Chili. Not a gourmet feast, but something.

When he came home, Ba closed his eyes and inhaled deeply. I thought I was home free when he took the first spoonful and made a little noise. I thought it meant he was happy. But now his question makes me think that I have misunderstood—maybe it was indigestion.

"Yes, Ba," I say. "I would." I try to make my voice serious, but not desperate. "Tryouts are this Saturday."

"It is a very big commitment, to play on a team. There are practices and games after school. And it would cut into your time for homework. Your grades are already not good." He doesn't even look at me. He bends his head down over the chili so I can see the top of his head, the whiteness of his scalp.

"I'm getting better. And I would make sure I got my homework done. Really," I say. If my teachers were here, they'd probably fall over in a collective faint. "I'm even doing better in math."

"I can help you with your work," says Ba.

I shake my head. "I don't need any help."

"Mark Santos, a boy in my class, he plays baseball *and* he gets all As," says Elaine.

"This is different," says Ba. "How would Peter get to practices?"

"Kids get rides with other kids' parents all the time," I point out.

Ba frowns. "You are so quick to impose on other people."

This is a big issue with Ba. *Imposing.*

"It's no big deal. Other families do stuff for each other all the time," says Elaine. "No one minds."

Ba pokes his fork in Elaine's direction. "We are different, Elaine." I wonder how he means we are different.

"I'll take care of everything," I say. "No one will think you're asking them to do anything." My stomach begins to burn.

Ba looks at me and then away. "Maybe next year," he says.

"I can't play next year," I say. My throat is tightening up. "I'll be too old."

Ba frowns. "You still have one more year."

"I'm twelve," I say. "I turned twelve in November." I didn't have a birthday party; I had not asked, and no one offered.

Ba is quiet for a moment. "Of course," he says. "You are twelve."

My father, who makes his living measuring out precise quantities of medicine, has forgotten how old I am.

There is a long silence, and then Elaine clears her throat. "Just for the record," she says. "I'm going to be eight on May 22."

Ba looks at both of us and smiles, barely. "You are both getting older."

Usually when my father makes a statement like this, it is followed by "and." As in, "And you should be acting more responsibly. And your grades are getting more important. And it's time to stop acting foolishly." But this time, that is all he says.

"Well?" I ask when it's clear he's not going to say anything else.

"Well what?"

"Can I play baseball? Can I go to tryouts?" I try to hold back the impatience in my voice.

Ba takes his time chewing his food.

"Yes," he says finally. "You may go to tryouts." Even though he is saying yes, I can still hear an undercurrent of no.

In the Before, I would have jumped out of my seat to hear Ba say that. But this is different.

"Thank you," I say. And then we go back to eating dinner, as if nothing has happened.

•CHAPTER•
TWELVE

IT'S SO EARLY THERE'S JUST A GRAYISH LIGHT OUTSIDE,
but I can't go back to sleep. It's the morning of tryouts.

I keep thinking about King Midas. He was this king
who wished that everything he touched would turn to
gold. He ended up not even being able to eat because
the food turned to gold, and he even turned his own
daughter to gold. Miss Gunderson, who told us the
story, said it was a parable about greed, but that doesn't
seem quite right. I think it is about making the right
wish. If King Midas had made a better wish, like, "I
wish I could turn things to gold only when I want
to," everybody would probably think he was a pretty
smart guy.

I close my eyes and make a wish. I wish that baseball
will make everything better.

It's a very simple wish.

. . .

Most of the dads are playing catch with the boys at the field. Because it is a warm spring day, a lot of them are wearing T-shirts and ball caps. Some of the dads are standing with their ball caps pulled down low, arms folded, watching the other players. They are probably the coaches, scouting out the players.

Ba isn't dressed like them. He is wearing a white button-down shirt and black pants, the way he does for work. He looks like someone from an old-time black-and-white movie, stuck in Technicolor.

"You don't have to stay," I say. "Just give me the money and I'll go register."

Ba shakes his head. "I think I should stay with you."

I start to walk faster. But Ba calls me back.

"Peter," he says. "Carry my bag." He is juggling a thermos, a bag filled with books and papers, and a stool.

I want to tell Ba that dads do not bring books to try-outs. They watch their sons play. But instead, I make up an excuse. "I have to go warm up."

"Very well," says Ba. He puts the stool, bag, and thermos on the ground and holds out his hands. "Let's warm up."

"What?" I look around to see if anyone is watching. "With you? You don't even have a glove."

Ba holds his hands in front of him, fingers apart. "You said you wanted to warm up. Let's warm up. Throw the ball."

I throw the ball with just enough speed that maybe it will make Ba want to stop. To my surprise, Ba catches the ball, moving his hands with a soft backward motion so that the ball won't bounce out. Then he throws the ball back at me, a grounder. I drop to my knees and block the ball.

"Stay on your feet," Ba tells me.

"I always catch the ball this way," I say. "It's fine." I know that I'm supposed to stay on my feet, but I didn't know that Ba did, too. I know how to play. I know a lot more about baseball than he does.

"Hey, Peter!" Sean runs up. "You decided to play! That's great!"

"Thanks." I hope he won't remind me of what I said earlier about playing.

Sean's face is already bright pink from the walk from the car. He is also wearing corduroys. They don't allow jeans at his school, so his mom doesn't buy him any.

"Are you ready?" I ask.

"Sure." Sean fans himself with his glove. "My old man can't believe I'm going to try out. He's really excited."

I look over at Ba. I am not sure what to say about him.

· · ·

During tryouts everything is done in fives. You hit five pitches, catch five throws, and throw each one back. You also run the bases while someone times you.

I do pretty well in the hitting and fielding. I whiff one ball, but hit two of the balls into the outfield. I don't miss any of the balls that are hit to me. I stay on my feet for the grounder, but when I look over, Ba is reading his book.

Running, though, is definitely my best event. It's hard to wait in line, to wait my turn to run the bases, and I keep jumping up and down to work off some energy and stay warm. While I'm waiting, one of the dads walks up to the guy with the timer.

"Dan Bennett! They letting you coach again?"

"Hey, Chuck. Yeah, I guess they ran out of drunks and parolees." The man with the timer laughs at his own joke, and then the two men shake hands. It is almost like a secret club, the way they talk to each other. I've never heard my father talk to anyone with that confidence and ease.

"Seriously, though, how many kids do you have from last year?"

"Oh, I've got over half the team coming back. I need to get me some live ones to fill in a few spots," says Mr.

Bennett. "Didn't see many kids last year who could get a piece of Rusty's fastball. Just need some kids who can score."

"Well," says Chuck, slapping Mr. Bennett on the back, "you are a credit to the league. That was some team you took to the division championship."

Championship? I try to get a better look at Mr. Bennett. He looks like a lot of dads out here—a little soft in the belly and wrinkly around the eyes. He has a thick brown mustache that jumps and wiggles when he talks. He must be something, though.

I imagine telling Mom we won the division.

How could she not answer back?

For that matter, I bet she would *come* to a championship game. She wouldn't miss it.

"Don't start your slide so far back," says Mr. Bennett to the kid in front of me. It is almost my turn. The kid's slide had ended a good two feet short of the base. Mr. Bennett looks at the stopwatch and shakes his head.

I laugh, mostly out of nervousness. Mr. Bennett looks at me and frowns.

"What, you think you're better than him?"

My heart almost stops beating. "Um, well, probably," I hear myself say.

"Um, well, probably." Mr. Bennett mimics me, using

a high voice. He writes down a time for the other kid. And then, before I have a chance to get set, he hits the button and says, "Prove it. Go!"

For a second, my feet scrabble to get traction in the hard, dry dirt. Then I take off for first base.

I adjust my stride slightly so I tag first with my right leg, pushing off slightly to change direction and head for second.

"Go, Peter, go!" someone yells. It sounds like Sean.

Faster. I imagine the ball coming in for the tag and lengthen my stride. Once I cross second, I swing wide and head for third. My legs begin to burn. I push through it.

I pretend that the third-base coach is giving me the go-ahead for home, his arm whipping around in a circle. *Go go go!*

We were told to slide at home, feet first. The trick to a really good slide is to keep your eyes on the bag the whole time. Nelson told me that. I slide across the plate, and then pop quickly to my feet.

Mr. Bennett clicks his stopwatch, and then half smiles, like he's pleased in spite of himself.

"Not bad, kid," he says. "Haven't seen too many times better than that. What's your name again?"

Yes. Now I have his attention.

• • •

Ba is not sitting with the other parents—he is sitting apart, on his stool, holding a Chinese newspaper. The pages of the newspaper are tissue thin, and threaten to blow away any second. It takes him a minute to notice me.

"Nixon's trip to China. It's very bad," he says. "Bad for Taiwan." He pokes at the paper with his index finger. "Now senators are being invited to China."

I don't say anything. I had seen the photos of Nixon's trip: President Nixon on the Great Wall, Mrs. Nixon admiring a row of roasted ducks. Ba probably hasn't seen anything I've done on the field.

Ba squints at me over the top of his newspaper.

"You would be faster running the bases if you picked up your feet a little bit," he says, putting down his paper. Ba looks over at the field. "Your friend Sean is about to have his turn." I can see him, too. He is two kids back from running.

"You should root for your friend," says Ba.

I walk over to the right-field fence, where some other kids are leaning over the fence, watching tryouts. One kid turns around and says, "Nice run."

"Thanks." I try to sound like it's no big deal.

Sean has only run a few feet when the laughter starts.

It starts with the kids waiting in line, and then ripples to the people standing near the field.

ZHWIT zhwit ZHWIT zhwit.

It is Sean. Apparently his legs are rubbing together when he runs, and the corduroy sounds like sawing wood. It doesn't help that Sean is not the most graceful runner.

"Look at him go!"

"Call the fire department! There's going to be a spontaneous combustion!"

"It's a miracle of nature. A whale's going to catch on fire!" That comment is from Martin Greer. He has an older brother who's been to juvie, and if you ask me, Martin's not far behind.

Sean's face goes from pink to bright red. I don't know if it is from the effort of running, or from the comments people are shouting at him. I step away from the fence.

After what seems like forever, Sean finally crosses home plate. He doesn't bother to slide. He bends over and puts his hands on his knees, gasping for breath. Mr. Bennett looks at him and wrinkles his nose, like something smells bad.

I turn away before Sean can see me. Probably the only thing more painful than watching Sean would be him knowing that I saw him.

• • •

When tryouts are over, I take my time packing up my equipment. I had heard that if you wait long enough, you can find out whose team you are on.

"We should go home," says Ba. He has finished his newspaper and is now reading one of his books. "We have been here a long time."

"Just a little longer," I beg. I have to know. Actually, it feels more like I am waiting for a confirmation. The more I think about it, the more I think I *have* to be on Bennett's team.

Sean comes up. I hadn't noticed it before, but his glove is brand new. "Hi, Mr. Lee," he says. "Hey, Peter, how did you do?"

"Hard to say." I don't want to make Sean feel bad. "Nice glove."

Sean looks at his glove as if he's remembering it's there for the first time. "Thanks," he says. "My dad was ready to buy out Sears, if you want to know the truth."

I look at Ba and try to imagine him wanting to buy anything sports related. I can't.

A man with a clipboard comes out of the dugout where all the coaches are meeting. "Folks," he said, "we're just about finished, but it looks like we have a few more players than we expected. If one of the dads is interested in coaching a team, we sure could use another coach to even things out."

No one says anything. I stare at Mr. Bennett. *Pick me.*

Sean leans over. "We should get on the same team, don't you think?" he says in a half whisper. "Since we live in the same neighborhood?"

"I'm not sure that's how they pick the teams," I whisper back. I can't imagine Dan Bennett picking Sean.

"As coach, of course, you get to coach your own boy." The man clears his throat. "My own son is going to age out next year, and I'm only sorry I didn't start coaching sooner."

It is kind of sad, the guy standing up there, asking for help with no one answering. Behind him, I can see Mr. Bennett moving around, talking to people.

"It really does create a better experience for the boys," says the man. "When the teams get too big, the kids don't get much playing time, it's harder to help them make adjustments in practice, that sort of thing."

A dad sitting a few feet away from me flips open a newspaper and begins working on a crossword puzzle. No one seems to be listening.

The man tries one more time. "We don't pay, of

course, but I promise you'll have memories you'll treasure for the rest of your lives. Good father–son memories— you can't buy those."

There is more silence, and then, someone speaks.

"I will," says a man to my left. "I will coach."

"Great!" says the guy. "I knew we'd get a taker. You won't regret it. And your name is?" He picks up the pencil that is attached to the clipboard with a string.

"Chen." I turn around, because Chen is my father's name, and I think it is amazing there is another person at tryouts with the same name.

· CHAPTER ·
THIRTEEN

I DON'T SAY ANYTHING WHEN BA JOINS THE COACHES'
meeting. Or when Ba makes me his first pick and finds
out that his team is named the Jaguars. Or when we walk
to the car and get in.

Once the car starts moving, though, I try to speak. It
feels like there is a hole in the middle of my chest, and
it is sucking away my words, the words I would have used
to explain to Ba that I already had plans.

"*You're* coaching." I say, finally. "*You're* coaching baseball."

"They said they needed another coach," says Ba. "I
can coach."

"You don't know how to coach baseball," I say. "You
don't even *like* baseball."

"I can learn," Ba says simply. Then he adds, "Your
friend Sean will be on the team. He will be helpful."

"What? You picked Sean?" I must have missed that.

"He is your friend," says Ba. "They said I had a free
pick, for friends and neighbors, that sort of thing. I

picked Sean. They said that we would do the rest of the drafts at another meeting."

I can't believe that Ba used his free pick on Sean. "He is only sort of my friend, and he's not very good," I say, remembering Sean's base running.

"He comes over quite a bit to our house," says Ba. "He's okay."

"What about your other friend, Chris?"

"What about him?"

Ba makes a funny motion with his mouth. "I have not seen him for a long time."

"He's busy."

"Did you see any good players during tryouts?" asks Ba. I shake my head.

"No? No good players?" says Ba.

I shake my head again. Ba shouldn't be asking me these questions. It's so clear that this is a bad idea, my father coaching. "People who are coaching usually know who is a good player and who is not," I say.

For a moment I think Ba is going to yell at me for speaking so rudely. I don't care. I am on the wrong team. I am supposed to be on Bennett's team. But instead, I am stuck on the wrong team with the wrong coach, who is going to pick all the wrong kids.

Somehow, I have made the wrong wish.

· CHAPTER ·
FOURTEEN

I FIND OUT ABOUT THE REST OF THE TEAM THE NEXT day when Martin Greer walks up to me and punches me in the arm. I have managed to go several grades without drawing Martin's attention, and the punch tells me that is about to change.

"You, what's your name? Peter?"

I nod.

He punches me again. "Whatsa matter? Are you a dummy? Can't talk?" Martin is half a foot taller than I am, and kind of meaty. I resist the urge to rub the spot he's punched.

I swallow. "I can talk."

"What's your last name?"

"Lee. It's Lee," I say.

"And your dad. His name is, like, Chung Lee?"

I have a brief internal debate on the merits of correcting someone like Martin on his Chinese pronunciation abilities, and decide to let it pass. "Something like that. A lot of people call him John."

The way Martin slams his fist into his other hand makes me think he was just using me to warm up. "I knew it! I got this phone call last night and the guy's all formal and stuff." Martin pretends to talk on the phone. "Ah, hello Martin. I am calling to introduce myself. I am Chung Lee, your baseball coach for this season." Of course, Martin sounds nothing like my father, but still, something about his impersonation is not completely off, either.

"Oh," I say, trying to ignore the fact that Martin is making fun of Ba. "You're on the team?"

"*My* rotten luck. What's a Chinaman know about baseball?"

I feel like saying, "Enough to win the Little League World Series, twice," but instead, I say, "Yeah, well, he picked you, didn't he?"

This stops Martin in his tracks. He squints at me for a minute as he tries to figure out whether or not I am insulting him or complimenting him.

"Do you know who else is on the team?" I decide to change the subject.

"Jimmy told me him and his brother Bobby were on the team," says Martin. "And I think Jimmy said something about Rickey Torres and Doug Levinger." He scratches his chin. "Not sure what Levinger is doing playing ball, but Torres has a decent bat."

Coming from Martin, any compliment about batting is big. That is because last summer, Martin managed to bust several windows of the music room hitting fungoes from the field below. The rumor was he was mad at the music teacher, Mrs. Springer, and he only got to come back to school because his grandfather paid to have all the windows replaced. Also, Martin goes to the library during music time now.

"Anyone else?" I ask. "You heard about anyone else?"

Martin punches me again. "What do I look like, the school newspaper? What's the matter, anyway? Shouldn't your dad be telling you these things?"

As much as I don't like Martin, I have to admit that he could hit a few things right on the head.

Sean comes over after school and tells me that a kid at his school named Danny Cooper is on the team. According to Sean, everyone calls him Coop and he likes to play shortstop.

"See?" says Sean. "I told you we'd be on the same team." Sean is so excited he looks like a puppy, all bright-eyed and eager. "I didn't know your dad could play ball."

"He can't. He didn't even grow up here."

This information does not dampen Sean's excitement. "Aw, it'll still be fun. We have some good players."

"Yeah, sure it will." Somehow, Sean thinks I am making a joke. He laughs and gives me a shove.

After Sean leaves, I look over the mail. There isn't much—a water bill and a reminder that Mom's *Family Circle* subscription is about to expire, but it gives me an excuse to talk to her about the team. It will be like talking about spring training, which she always loved. Spring training, she said, was hope and promise, laid out on a baseball field.

"There's a bunch of kids from my school, including some big hitters. We should be good on offense." That's as close as I want to get to talking about Martin Greer, specifically. I wait for her response.

But there isn't one. In fact, I'm not sure she even heard me. Her eyes are open, but she seems to be somewhere else.

"Sean's on the team," I tell her. Maybe it will help to mention someone she knows. "He's slow, but that's okay. There's another kid from his school who's on our team. Sean says he's awesome at short."

Mentioning shortstop should make Mom happy—she loved to hear about Gene Alley and Mazeroski turning double plays.

But the bait doesn't work this time, though she does respond with a low *hmmm*.

I keep going. I try to think of all the good parts to talk about, which means that I don't talk about Ba coaching. I tell her I like the name Jaguars, and that the best team color to get was navy blue or green. I ramble through my ideas on batting order and stealing home. I feel like I'm fishing, trying to bait the hook with something that will get Mom's attention. But she's not biting. When I run out of things to talk about, I ask Mom if she is going to eat dinner with us.

"Not tonight," says Mom.

"Maybe tomorrow?" I suggest.

From the way Mom closes her eyes, you would think tomorrow was a very long way away.

·CHAPTER·
FIFTEEN

WE HAVE OUR FIRST PRACTICE ON FRIDAY, AFTER SCHOOL.
Ba arranged to trade hours at the pharmacy with someone, and he picked up Sean and me to drive to the field.

It's not a particularly nice field—it's just a scrubby
practice field, with crabgrass and sloppy dirt paths. Ba
tells us to walk around the field and pick up any litter
while he brings up some of the equipment.

Sean and I walk to opposite ends of the outfield—
Sean to the right, me to the left. When I reach down to
pick up a Hershey bar wrapper, though, I'm suddenly hit
by the feeling of how wrong this all is. I'm not supposed
to be here with Ba or Sean. I should be here with Nelson.
And then I remember all over again that I can't.

The field narrows and drops away, and I feel like I'm
on a precipice. At any moment, I could fall or fly away to
nothingness. Anywhere but here. For what must be the
thousandth time, I think, *Why aren't you here?* It's almost

like a math problem—if I can come up with the right answer, I can make him come back.

I can't do this; I can't. I can't make it through a whole season like this.

But I have to. This is all I have.

I reach down and pretend to look for more garbage, but what I'm really doing is pulling at the blades of grass, hoping they're strong enough to hold me to the earth.

Then there's a hand on my shoulder, warm and heavy. It's Sean.

"You want to throw a couple, before the real practice starts?"

I stand up straight and try to look normal, like all I've been doing is picking up trash, but I'm grateful for the weight of Sean's hand on my shoulder, keeping me from flying away. I nod. Sean gives me a friendly pat, and then jogs to the dugout to get our gloves. I try to put all my energy into throwing and catching, feeling the snap of the ball in my glove, making each throw as perfect as I can. Slowly, I feel my heartbeat return to normal.

Sometimes I think about what I would do if I had one more day with Nelson, what we would do. We'd want to eat all of our favorite foods, of course, and I'd want Nelson to tell me more things, the things he always said

I'd understand better when I got older. But most of all, I'd want to make sure we'd do this—we'd get to play some ball, and he'd show me that palmball, one more time.

After most of the kids show up, Ba assigns us to different positions in the field, including me at third. The he begins hitting grounders to first. He is surprisingly good at hitting the ball to where he wants it to go. He has a large bucket of balls with him at home plate, and he hits one after another. All the balls go to Coop, who's at first.

"When is he going to hit some out this way?" I hear one of the players ask.

I try to act like this is perfectly normal, but after another dozen grounders, still to Coop, the other kids start looking at me, as if it is my job to say something.

I ask Ba how many more grounders he's going to hit to Coop. I expect him to say something like he'll get to us in just a minute, or even hit one to another player.

"Eighteen," replies Ba, without looking at me.

"Eighteen!" I don't know how Ba came up with that number. "Is anyone but the first baseman getting practice today?"

"You will each field forty grounders," says Ba.

"This is boring," says Yonder. He's one of the kids who doesn't go to my school or Sean's school. He wore sandals to practice and had to borrow a glove, which does not bode well.

"It does not matter if practice is, as you say, boring," says Ba. "What matters is that you have a way to improve."

For a moment, there is silence. And then Aaron, the other kid who is from a different school, shouts out from shortstop, "C'mon, then! If we're each getting forty grounders, let's see who's the best! You, first base. How many have you missed?" Aaron is short and skinny, and has a high, singsongy voice. He is constantly moving around—adjusting his cap, swinging his arms, hitching up his pants.

"Three, maybe four," says Coop.

"Four," says Doug Levinger. "Definitely four."

Coop turns and scowls at Doug.

"Okay then!" says Aaron. "We're going to keep track of how many each player misses." He punches his glove.

Aaron's idea seems to make everyone less restless, except for Coop, who doesn't seem to like that we're all keeping count of his mistakes. When Coop misses the next grounder, Bobby Lattimore yells, "Five!" from right field, and Coop threatens to bean him.

Eventually, Ba makes his way around the entire field. First base, second base, shortstop, and third, and then the outfield from right to left. By the time he's done, we all have a pretty good idea of who are the good fielders, and who aren't. Doug and Sean have the most mistakes; they each flub fourteen. Coop and Aaron do the best; Coop missed five, and Aaron missed four. I missed ten, though I think Ba hit them a little harder to me.

No one counts out loud when Ba hits the last grounder to Yonder in left field, but I'm pretty sure we're all counting in our heads. When Ba hits the fortieth grounder, we all sigh and look at each other, wondering what will happen next. Maybe we'll get to scrimmage or do something interesting.

Ba picks up a ball out of the bucket and hits it up high toward the pitcher's mound.

"Now," he says. "Forty fly balls."

Halfway through the fly ball drill, a station wagon pulls into the parking lot and someone gets out. The car takes off, kicking up dust behind it.

It is Martin Greer. I'd kind of hoped that he had decided to quit the team.

He walks slowly up to the field, like he isn't nearly an hour late. Ba doesn't even notice him until he practically hits Martin with the bat.

"You are late," says Ba, shouldering the bat.

"Don'tcha even want to know who I am first?" asks Martin. Ba hasn't asked any of the kids what their names are. He calls most of them "you."

"You are late," repeats Ba.

Martin looks at Ba for a moment, and then points at the field. "Where do you want me to play?"

"You can play in the outfield *after* you do twenty push-ups and five laps around the field," says Ba. "That is the penalty for being late."

Martin throws his glove onto the ground. "That's bull. It wasn't my fault."

"It is unfair to your team for you to be late," says Ba calmly. He raises his voice slightly. "*Anyone* who is late must do twenty push-ups and five laps around the field."

From the players' faces, I'm sure some of them are thinking, *Maybe twenty push-ups and five laps isn't so bad compared to standing around watching people catch fly balls.*

Martin spends another few moments glaring at Ba. Then he walks off to the side and begins doing push-ups. As soon as he is done with his laps, Ba begins hitting the balls to him.

The first practice feels like it's never going to end.

·CHAPTER·
SIXTEEN

THE NEXT DAY AT SCHOOL, I WONDER WHAT *MY* PEN-alty is going to be for Martin getting extra laps and push-ups from Ba. I don't have to wait long.

"Lee," says Martin, backing me up against the slide during recess. "Your dad runs one bad practice. Bad Lee, get it? Badly."

I'm not sure what to say. It *had* been a boring prac-tice. By the time everyone had finished their fielding drills, we only had fifteen minutes to scrimmage and do something like real baseball. The rest of the season just can't be like this.

"We need some batting practice. That defensive stuff is boring as all get out." Maybe practice is extra boring for Martin because it is easy for him; he missed the few-est balls. Between grounders and fly balls, he only missed two grounders and two fly balls.

Rickey Torres walks up. "You guys talking about practice last night?"

"What'd you think, Torres?" Martin shifts his weight and spits on the ground.

Rickey shrugs. "My dad's always saying I need to work on my fielding, so I guess it was okay. It was just kind of boring, except for the scrimmaging at the end." He looks at me. "No offense."

I put up a hand. "Don't worry about it."

"So, what're you going to do about this situation, Lee?" asks Martin. "Are we going to get some hitting in next time?"

"Yeah," says Rickey. He takes a swing with an imaginary bat. "Now you're talking!"

"I'll let Ba know," I say. "About the hitting."

"Who?" Martin leans one ear toward me, like he has suddenly become hard of hearing.

"Ba. My father. I call him Ba."

"Baaaaaaawwwwwww?" Martin stretches and exaggerates the sound. "What kind of name is that?"

"It's Chinese." I try to sound serious and important, but part of me is wishing I had just said "my father."

"Aw." Rickey looks at me and then looks away. "It's all right."

It is not all right with Martin. "*Baaaaaaaaa.* How do you know a goat won't come instead of your dad?"

I glare at Martin and wish I had a good comeback.

"Shut up," I say.

"How do you say 'shut up' in Chinese? Is it *ching chang chong?*"

I turn and begin walking away. *Just walk away*, I tell myself, *because the kid who throws the first punch always gets in the most trouble.* Nelson told me that.

"Hey!" Martin yells at me. "Don't forget to talk to your dad!"

I wait until the night before the next practice before talking to Ba. We are halfway through dinner before I bring it up. Laney is going on and on about a goldfinch she saw.

"It was so beautiful!" she said. "It must have been a male, because it was this bright, bright shade of yellow. And the call—"

If Laney gets started on making a birdcall, she won't stop, so I interrupt. "Uh, Martin told me that he was hoping that we'd get some batting practice in." Actually, I could never imagine Martin using a word like *hoping*. Ba's forehead immediately wrinkles up.

"Martin? Who is Martin?" asks Ba.

"That really big kid with the brown hair," I tell him. Since Ba is still frowning, I add, "The kid who came late and had to do push-ups."

"Oh yes! Martin. Is he one of your friends at school? Do you talk a lot?"

No to friends. *No* to talking. "Something like that," I say.

Ba evidently thinks "something like that" means yes. "And the other boys, they are your friends, too?" He stops eating and leans forward a bit.

I'm not sure what the point of this question is. "Sure. Sure they are. We're all *pals*."

"Good." Ba completely misses my sarcasm. "You should *all* be friends, because you're all on the same team."

"Okay." I say *okay* so it is half-word, half-sigh. Like most conversations with Ba, I think we're talking about one thing, and it turns into a lecture about something else.

"Tell your *friends* I am planning to have batting practice tomorrow," Ba says.

"The goldfinch call sounds like it's saying *po-ta-to chip*," announces Laney.

The next day when we get to the field, Ba tells me to get the equipment bag out of the trunk of the car. It's really heavy, and when I drop it in the dugout, I figure out why. About a half-dozen bats and helmets come spilling out of the bag. The helmets tumble out like boulders, while the bats roll on the ground in small arcs.

One of the bats is a Louisville Slugger with red tape on the handle.

It's Nelson's.

I'd know that bat anywhere. Even if I didn't see the notches, I'd recognize the way the tape is peeling off the handle. I run my fingers over the notches, silently adding one. It should say fifty-three. Fifty-three home runs.

I don't know how Nelson's bat ended up here, instead of packed away with everything else, but I am grateful. I feel like I've run into an old friend.

"Peter, arrange the bats along the third-base line," says Ba. "And get the bucket of balls." He is standing at home plate, making notes on a clipboard.

I wonder if Ba would know what the notches stood for if I showed him the bat. I wonder if he even knows this was Nelson's.

When Ba isn't looking, I take the bat and lay it in the tall grass, along the fence behind the dugouts. The fence is supposed to separate the Port-o-Potties from the rest of the field, but no one comes back here—everyone uses the woods. I'll come get it later, and then I'll put it away, somewhere safe.

Ba places a batting helmet next to each bat. He doesn't notice that one is missing. After all the kids have arrived, including Martin, he has us warm up, and then we sit on the ground, waiting.

"Today, we are going to work on the correct batting stance and swing," Ba announces. He holds up a book. "We will be following the advice of this book. I would like Aaron, Sean, Jimmy, Martin, and Bobby to stand up and take a bat."

The guys he called stand up and pick up a bat. Ba asks them all to take a batting stance. Bobby is a lefty, so he stands slightly away from the others so he won't knock bats with them. Then Ba shows us the front of his book. It says, *The Young Man's Guide to Baseball*.

Ba begins by reading about how a hitter should keep his head still while he is in a batting position. Actually, Ba doesn't say "hitter," he says "batsman" because that's what the book says. A couple of kids smirk when he reads *batsman* for the first time, because it sounds like Batman.

Then Ba goes on to read about the importance of a good stance and a good swing. At this point, some of the guys start putting their bats on the ground because they're tired of waiting, but Ba doesn't notice. He keeps reading. We might as well be in school. I keep hearing words that make sense—weight change, balance, timing— but I can't force myself to listen to the sentences; they are so boring. Coop rolls on the ground and lets out a small moan.

Ba is about to read the section on swing when Martin interrupts.

"Are you going to read to us all day? Or are we actually going to get to take a *swing* during *batting* practice?"

I look at Ba, who is still holding up the book. I'm kind of expecting the world to explode because no one speaks to Ba like that. Instead, though, Ba nods and closes his book.

"Of course," he says. "By all means. Take a swing."

Martin takes the first swing, and the other guys quickly follow suit. My father watches silently for a few swings.

"Martin and Aaron have good, level swings," he finally announces. "Sean, you need to time your swing with your step. Bobby, keep your elbow in on your swing—you will get more power that way. Jimmy, you are moving your head."

I can't believe Ba actually noticed that much. But when everyone takes the next swing, I can see that Ba is right. Sean needs to take a longer stride. And even though he is swinging at imaginary balls, Jimmy is jerking his head back right before he swings.

I can't figure out how my father has learned so much about baseball so quickly.

"Let me guess," says Martin. "Thirty-eight more swings."

"Close," says Ba. "Eighteen more."

Martin shakes his head, but he keeps swinging. "Any chance we'll get to swing at, you know, an actual ball?"

"Soon," says Ba. "Soon."

When the first group finishes, it is time for the second group to go. I get into my stance, suddenly feeling very conscious of the fact that Ba might see things that are wrong with my swing that I didn't know about. The bat I wound up with feels heavy, and the handle is oddly thick. I think of Nelson's bat over in the grass.

"Swing!" barks Ba. We all take a swing. I make mine as perfect as I can, but it's not perfect enough.

"Peter," says Ba. "You're not focusing on the ball."

This is true, I suppose. I was thinking of Nelson's bat. But still, I defend myself. "There is no ball," I point out. "How can you tell I'm not focused when the ball isn't there?"

"I'm watching your eyes," says Ba. "You're not *imagining* the ball."

I want to say, "How can you tell what I'm imagining?" Instead I say, "I've never had a problem making contact." This is better than arguing directly with Ba.

Ba makes a little noise in his throat but doesn't talk to anyone else in the group, which is not fair. I'm not even close to being the worst member of our group. I can't figure out why Ba is picking on me. My group has Doug Levinger, who looks like he is *afraid* of the imaginary ball and chokes up on the bat so far he has about six inches left. I take another batting stance and wipe my face on my sleeve.

Even though there is a light spring breeze, I might as well be swinging through thick, hot soup. I can barely see, and with each swing, Ba seems to find something new to pick on. "Turn your hips. Drop your back elbow." And every time I fix one thing, two new problems spring up.

I just need to get through practice, and get Nelson's bat. That's my real job today. When practice is over, I'll get the bat and slide it into the long dark space under the row of front seats in the car. Then, when we get home, I'll put it in a safe place where no one will ever find it.

When practice is finally over, I wait until Ba is talking to one of the other parents, and then I slip over to the fence. I even have an alibi if someone asks me what I'm doing over there. I'll say that I'm looking for foul balls.

I walk to the exact spot where I left it. I had been sure to check for landmarks. Three fence posts from the right, next to a large clump of wild daisies.

A perfect hiding place.

It's gone.

• CHAPTER •
SEVENTEEN

IT'S GONE.

I'm going to throw up. I swallow hard and force myself to look more carefully. *Think*. I walk up and down the fence line in short steps, dragging my feet through the long grass, even in places I know it can't possibly be. I get down on my knees and thrust my hands into the grass, scraping my fingers against the chain-link fence.

It's gone.

I blink my eyes and force myself to focus. Someone must have taken it when I wasn't looking, when I was in the middle of the world's most stupid batting practice. People do walk along the road. Someone could have walked in closer to the field, maybe to watch practice or use the latrine. They could have seen the bat and taken it.

Idiot, idiot, idiot.

"Peter! What are you doing over there? Help carry the equipment," Ba calls to me.

I hesitate a moment, wondering if I should tell Ba

what has happened. I try to think of a version of the truth that will create the fewest questions. *I think one of the bats ended up over here, and I'm looking for it.* I try to calculate how helpful Ba would be, in the event he actually decided to help me look.

In the end, though, I say nothing. He won't help me. And no matter what I say, I doubt he'll understand what's really missing.

On the way home, I try not to think about the bat because every time I do, I feel like I'm being punched in the chest. It's hard not to think about batting, though, because Ba won't stop talking about it.

"You need to work on your feet. Watch the placement of your feet, relative to home plate."

"Uh-huh."

"And your hands. You tend to choke up on the bat."

Bat.

"Your left elbow is coming up too high."

I sigh noisily. "How do you know so much about baseball, anyway?" I say. "You learned all of that from *The Young Man's Guide to Baseball*?"

Ba looks at me, surprised. "I played when I was a boy."

"What? In Taiwan?" It's my turn to be surprised. For a moment, the pain over the lost bat lessens.

"Yes, in Taiwan." He wrinkles his brow. "Where do you think those boys in Williamsport learned to play?"

"I know about *them*, it's just that..." It's hard to explain. The Taiwan my father talks about and the Taiwan those boys live in seem like two very different places in my mind.

"You know, when the Japanese occupied Taiwan, they used baseball to encourage the students to learn the ways of the Japanese."

"The Japanese? Baseball?" Ba must have gotten confused somewhere.

"Baseball is a national sport of Japan," says Ba, as if I should have known. "They encouraged the formation of teams in Taiwan." His voice softens. "The Taiwanese kids, some of them, did not want us there, the kids from the mainland. They would follow us around, throw rocks at us, call us names, and fight. I decided I had to play their game, better than they did." He hesitates, and then adds, "I would practice instead of doing homework."

Until now, I had thought Ba must have been the perfect, hardworking student—that is, when I remembered that he had once been a kid at all.

"The game we played was a little different from baseball, but mostly the same. Instead of pitching, we would put a ball, a little rubber ball, on the end of a board and snap it up with the foot, like a lever. Then, *pah!*" Ba pretends to swing a bat.

"I practiced my swing every morning and every night," says Ba. "I analyzed every swing, trying to improve. When I decided I was ready, I joined their game, and I got a home run on my first at bat." For a moment, Ba is not seeing the road. "Bases loaded, two outs." Ba slowly rubs his hand over his mouth. I think he is erasing a smile. "They left me alone after that."

"If you could do all that, why did you read from a book?" Part of me still can't believe Ba played baseball. Before he became the coach, he had never played catch with me or Nelson. Never tossed balls for us to hit. Never stopped to listen to a Pirates game or picked up a sports page.

"The book is written by an expert. The book should be the best," Ba says simply.

Then I ask the question I really want to ask. "All this time, why didn't you play with us?"

Ba adjusts his hands on the steering wheel. "I became a man, Peter. A man, a husband, a father, in a different country. A man in this situation does not play the games of a child."

"You're playing now," I point out.

"I am coaching," Ba corrects me. "I am coaching my son."

· CHAPTER ·
EIGHTEEN

"I'VE BEEN TALKING TO SOME KIDS ON OTHER TEAMS," Martin says to me in the dugout after practice one day. We are all in there, waiting, because Ba says we need to have a team meeting, but first he needs to get something from the car. "Your dad's practices are longer *and* more boring than anyone else's. That's a fact. No one else spends so much time working on swinging at imaginary balls. We're going to get clobbered next week."

I think about Ba, and his story about perfecting his swing, but there's no way I'm telling that story to Martin. And no one else says anything, which in a way is even worse than accusations. It's like practice is so awful that it's not worth pretending.

"He's doing his best," says Aaron. "That's all you can ask of anyone." I silently thank Aaron for defending Ba, so I don't have to.

" 'He's doing his best,' " says Martin, mimicking Aaron. "That's what losers say about other losers to make them feel better about being losers." He stares out into the field.

I don't have it in me to argue with Martin today. I keep thinking of Nelson's bat, and hating myself for losing it. I don't know what's worse—never having it, or having it for only a moment.

We're not the only grumpy team in baseball. I heard on the radio this morning that the Pirates, while down at spring training, voted to strike. Something about retirement, I think. This has never happened before, so there's no telling how long this will take. Which means no baseball, at least for anyone who isn't watching Little League.

"We'll be lucky to win one game," predicts Martin.

"You don't know that," says Aaron. "We haven't even played our first game."

I've been thinking that if Mom came to a couple of games, she would really and truly start to feel better. She would smell the freshly cut grass and feel the sun on her face. She'd remember how your heart lifts when you hear the crack of a hit that's a home run.

But, of course, the most important thing is having a winning team to root for.

"Don't need to play a game to know how bad we are," says Martin, half to Aaron, half to himself. "Like you."

He points at Sean. "You are a terrible catcher. You might as well play for the other team."

Sean shifts. "I'm still getting used to the position. My dad told me that playing catcher is good for someone my size." Sean is the only one who has volunteered to catch, and it's true, he's struggling. A lot of balls are getting by him during practice; balls that will turn into runs during games.

"You're a big target, all right," mutters Martin. "That's why you're catcher."

Some of the players laugh, but it's an uncomfortable laugh. Everyone likes Sean, but no one wants to cross Martin, including me.

"Lay off," says Aaron. "It's not like you know everything about baseball." The two eye each other.

Martin turns his head to the right and spits. "What's there to know? Three strikes and you're out. Three outs and the inning's over." He gives some of the other guys a what-an-idiot look.

"Three strikes and you're out?" asks Aaron.

"Of course." A couple of guys laugh with Martin.

"Actually." I am surprised to hear my own voice, but I know where Aaron is going. "If the catcher loses control of the ball on the third strike . . ."

126

Aaron takes over. ". . . the batter can take off for first. Might still get thrown out, but he can run."

Together, Aaron and I have shut up Martin for a moment. It feels good. "How 'bout this one?" asks Aaron. "How do you get a one-man triple play?"

"That's easy," says Rickey. "Ball pops up, player catches the ball, say, over by second. First out. Meanwhile, runner on second doesn't see the catch, and gets tagged out when he steps off the base. Likewise, runner on first gets tagged trying to come into second. One-two-three."

"You can have any kind of play if the other players are dumb enough," says Martin.

For once, though, no one is interested in what Martin has to say. "Do another one," says Sean.

"Okay," I say. "How about a *no*-man triple play?"

The dugout goes silent. Then Aaron says, "Can't do it. That's impossible."

Nelson had told me this one. I savor the words, trying to sound like Nelson when I say them. "It's not impossible. First off, you have to know the infield fly rule. Runners on first and second, and the batter pops up, short. Umpire calls it out on the infield fly rule."

I continue, "Meanwhile, the runner on first tries to

run, but on the way, he passes the runner on second. He's out."

"Yeah, okay," says Aaron, nodding.

"The ball comes down from its pop fly and beans the runner who's leaving second. Now he's out. Triple play."

"Stoo-pid," pronounces Martin.

"No, that's cool," says Aaron, and I know he gets it. This isn't about whether any of these plays will ever actually happen. It's a question of whether it's even possible.

"Yeah, that's really neat," adds Doug. Doug usually doesn't say anything; he's the quiet type, a little nervous.

"Sheesh, Levinger, you sound like a girl," snorts Martin. *"That's really NEAT!"*

Some of the guys laugh, but I won't do anything that makes Martin look good. I notice that Aaron doesn't join in, either. Martin and the Lattimores laugh and flip their hands in the air, saying, "Really NEAT!" Doug looks away.

"And worse," says Martin, playing to the larger group, "Dougie here *throws* like a girl, too."

There's some more laughing, but then suddenly, it stops.

"What is going on here?" Ba is standing in the doorway.

No one answers.

"I expect you all to conduct yourselves as gentlemen at all times," says Ba. He hefts a large bag onto the floor of the dugout. "Especially when you are in uniform."

"Uniforms!" shouts Aaron. "Yes!" We've all been waiting for uniforms.

Everyone crowds around the bag.

"I hope we got red, or green. They're the best colors," says Jimmy.

"Yeah, if you're a Christmas tree," says Bobby.

"Black and gold, black and gold," chants Coop.

"*Everyone* wants those colors," says Martin. "We won't get them."

Yonder reaches into the bag and yanks out a shirt. "They're . . . brown?"

"Brown?!" says Sean. He holds up a shirt and a loud groan goes up from the whole team. The uniform is the plainest medium brown.

"Please do not grab," says Ba. He pulls everything out of the bag, and arranges them in neat piles on the dugout bench. The shirt, the pants, and the hats are all brown. The socks are yellow, and the writing on the shirts matches the socks.

"It's the color of . . ." starts Jimmy.

"Mud," finishes Bobby. "A scab. Mom's coffee."

"Are you kidding me?" says Martin. "I think I stepped in this color this morning." He glares at me, as if this is my fault.

"Brown is a very practical color," says Ba. "Any stains should blend right in. It will make laundry less difficult."

Aaron picks up a shirt and looks at it. "It's not so bad. At least we have uniforms."

"You also need to, uh, get your supporters," says Ba. He holds up a smaller box and rattles it around. "Please wear them to the game."

"Are they all the same?" asks Doug, reaching into the box.

"Sorry, no *extra small*," cracks Martin.

"They're all the same size. Just take one," says Aaron, grabbing one.

Ba waits until everyone stops making wisecracks. Then he says, "Our first game is Saturday at ten. Please arrive an hour early to warm up."

· CHAPTER ·
NINETEEN

BA IS WORKING AT THE KITCHEN TABLE, ASSIGNING positions and drawing up the batting order. Like everything else he does, it's all orderly and carefully done. He has made a grid, with the positions written in columns across the top, and the innings in rows down the left-hand side. He puts a clean, blank piece of paper under his hand so he does not smudge his chart.

I take a quick peek over his shoulder.

"You're putting *Doug* at first?" I say, pointing at the first column. "For three innings? Doug is one of the worst fielders we have."

"Yes, I know," says Ba, not moving to change the assignment.

"What do you mean, you know? If you *know*, then you don't put him at first."

"Doug needs the practice," says Ba.

"Practice is for practice. Games are for winning."

Ba pinches his mouth into a tight line. "I was told at the coaches' meeting that our primary goal is player development. Winning should be the natural result of that improvement."

I think about Dan Bennett at tryouts. I don't think he was looking for players to *improve.*

"Maybe you could put Doug in for one inning, when we've got a decent lead. But Bobby or maybe Aaron should go there. Bobby's a lefty, and Aaron's got a real sure glove." I see Ba hesitate. "Doug's gonna get creamed until he feels more comfortable at first."

That's enough to persuade Ba. He takes his white gum eraser, and carefully erases DOUG from first base. Then he uses his mechanical pencil to print BOBBY in the boxes for the first three innings, and AARON for the fourth and fifth, and DOUG for the last inning.

Ba has put Rickey and Jimmy in for second base, so I skip over that column. At shortstop, though, I look for Coop's name, but instead see Yonder for three innings. A little more searching reveals that Coop has been stuck in right field for three innings, and then third for three innings.

"You gotta have Coop at short," I say. "No one can play short the way he can."

"No one else *will learn* to play shortstop if we don't let them."

I think about Yonder, standing in left field, barely paying attention. I'm pretty sure that playing ball was not his idea.

"I'll bet he doesn't even know what plays to call out in different situations," I say. "You should at least warn him that he's going to play short so he'll pay attention. And he should pay attention to what Coop is doing."

And so it goes, me and Ba going over his chart, position by position, with me arguing over and over that putting our worst players in the most important positions is not a great idea. It's like Ba *wants* us to lose.

And as for me, I need to know we're going to play decently before I invite Mom to a game. We have to have at least a *chance* of winning.

Then, in the second to last column, we get to PITCHER.

"Ah," says Ba triumphantly, sliding the paper to reveal the assignments. "Now, here I have done what you wanted me to. I have only put in players who can actually pitch. It is only what is fair to the other team."

I look down, and for a second, I cannot even process what my name is doing there.

"You have me pitching? I never said I wanted to pitch. I've never even pitched in practice." My voice crawls upward, desperate.

"We only have a few players who can pitch consistently," says Ba. "Martin, Aaron, and you. I'm sure as the season progresses, more players will be able to pitch."

When I think about pitching, I think about Nelson and hydrangea petals that fall like snow. I think about that palmball that Nelson promised to teach me.

I shake my head. "I'll play any other position."

I think about my wish, my simple wish that baseball would make everything better. I wonder how this all got so complicated.

Ba pulls his head back and stares at me. "You can pitch. I have seen you." He says this as if he does not know that happened in the Before, and that we live in the After.

I blink, hard. "I don't, not now."

Ba sighs and studies his piece of paper.

I think of an option, one that will keep me safely away from pitching. "Look," I say. "I'll *catch*."

This makes Ba pause for a moment. Right now, Sean is the only person catching because everyone else has pretty much outright refused. Sean is miserable at catcher, always complaining about his knees and groaning when he has to stand up and chase a ball that's gone past him into the backstop, which is often.

"You know," says Ba, "Americans like to put the big boys at catcher. But did you notice the Taiwanese team? They put small, quick players at catcher."

I nod, not because I knew this, but because I think it will get me what I want. "So, can I catch instead?"

Ba taps his paper a few times, and then begins erasing the column marked CATCHER. He flicks away the crumbs.

"The team could use another catcher," he says shortly. "Fine. Catch."

·CHAPTER·
TWENTY

BA AND I GET READY EARLY FOR THE GAME BECAUSE we have to get the field prepped. After I put on my uniform, I take my black band off my shirt from yesterday, and begin to pin it to my shirt for today.

And then I stop.

I turn to the mirror and hold up the black band, first on one side, and then the other. I can't make it look right. For one, if I put it where I normally wear it, it covers up the writing on the shirt. And two, as bad as the uniform looks, it looks even worse with the black band.

I put the band down, and look at the shirt with no band. It's like looking at one of Laney's books that's cut into sections, where you can mix and match the faces and bodies. Elaine used to crack herself up, putting a ballerina body with a fireman head, or an astronaut head with an ice skater body. The face is my face, but the shirt looks like it belongs to someone else.

But it also looks okay. I mean, it looks like a baseball uniform—a regular uniform like everyone else's. And that's the point. We're supposed to look alike—unified.

There is a small back pocket in the pants. I fold the band once, in half, and then I put it in my pocket.

On my way out of the house, I stop in the living room.

"We have our first game today," I say to Mom. I open my arms, so she can see the whole uniform. I wonder if she'll notice what's missing.

I'll take anything. A lifted eyebrow. A bright look in her eyes. A *Well, look at you.*

If she looks the least interested, I tell myself, *I'll invite her to come to the game right now.*

Mom turns ever so slightly in my direction. You might have missed it if you weren't looking carefully. She turns her far shoulder just a little bit, twisting from the waist.

"Okay," she says. "Bye."

I'll wait.

Ba and I get to the field first. Ba finds two rakes, and we work on the infield, making the dirt smooth and taking out the rocks.

When Aaron comes running up, it's still early. He grins and waves.

"Game day! Yes! Let's go, Jaguars!" Aaron punches the air. "We're going to demolish the other team! Look out . . . look out . . ." Aaron pauses in the middle of his one-man pep rally. "Um, what's their name? The other team?"

Ba smiles the tiniest smile. "The Hornets."

"Oh yeah! The Jaguars are going to swat the Hornets away!" Aaron yanks a bat out of his bag, and takes a big swing with it. "Swat!"

Aaron's bat is a Louisville Slugger with red tape on the handle.

Aaron sees me staring and stops. "What?"

I reach out to take it, but then stop myself. "Is that yours? Where did you get it?"

Aaron gets a funny look, guarded and suspicious. "I found it."

"By the fence? Near the latrine?"

"Yeah." Suddenly, Aaron's face changes. "Hey—is it yours?" Aaron holds the bat out to me. "I asked around, but no one claimed it."

I take the bat and automatically turn it around so I can see the notches. I run my thumb over them, feeling them against my skin.

"What are those for?" asks Aaron.

"Home runs."

"Wow! You hit all those home runs?"

"No, not me." And then, before I can stop the words, "My brother did."

"You have a brother that plays, too, huh?" asks Aaron.

Now I feel stuck between a truth and a lie. Because it *is* Nelson's, but I'm letting Aaron think that Nelson is alive, maybe about to come watch the game any minute now.

"He died last September," I add. Then I wait. I wonder what Aaron thinks now.

Aaron's eyes widen. "I'm sorry," he says. "I saw you were wearing a black band before, but I figured it was for a grandparent or something."

My hand goes up to the place where the band would have been. I mumble something about the uniform. I reach back and touch the band in my pocket, just to make sure it's still there.

I wait for Aaron to look away, or say that he is sorry for my loss, but instead he says, "He must have been a really good ballplayer."

"Nelson," I say. "Nelson was the best." I clear my throat. "He was the one who told me about running on a third strike." I force myself to process this moment. I'm not wearing my black band. I'm talking about Nelson. Everything is still okay.

"Yeah," says Aaron. "Most of the stuff I know about baseball is from my older brothers. Travis is seventeen, and Larry is fifteen."

"Nelson was eighteen, almost nineteen," I tell him. And then I realize that one day, I'll be older than Nelson. But in my mind, he'll always be older than me.

Then we both look down at the ground, looking for something to say.

"Do you want to warm up?" asks Aaron finally.

"Okay," I say. I start putting on the catcher's gear.

And it is okay. Actually, being able to talk about Nelson and then do something normal is more than okay.

Aaron's dad walks up and hands the scoring book and a slip of paper to Aaron. "Put the batting order in for me, will you? I need to get my chair out of the car."

I watch Aaron fill in the blanks for a few minutes. Something's not quite right, though.

"You know, something's different about you."

"Me? No, not really." Aaron doesn't look at me, but grips the pen more tightly.

"Yeah, you." I watch Aaron for a few moments more. "Oh, I know what it is—you're left-handed!" Aaron's hand curls around the words, trying not to smear them.

"Oh, that." Aaron relaxes and looks at me. "Sheesh, you don't have to be so dramatic. I thought you were going to say something really awful."

"But you pitch right-handed. And bat right, too."

"Don't remind me." Aaron leans back and adjusts his cap. "My dad would love for me to be a left-handed pitcher, but for whatever reason, I play baseball right-handed."

"It'd be better the other way around. You know, a righty who plays left?"

Aaron shrugs. "Have you noticed that most of life isn't straightforward? You know? There are always complications."

I know. I know that people see me and see a regular kid, but I don't feel like one, not anymore. But telling Aaron about Nelson and knowing that Aaron is okay with that feels good. Not complicated.

·CHAPTER·
TWENTY-ONE

WE DON'T GET OFF TO THE BEST START. AS THE HOME team, we pitch first. After the first batter gets a single on the second pitch, Ba calls time-out and waves his arm at me and Aaron.

"Peter, don't you see me signaling you?"

"What?"

"Signals, Peter. You should look to me for a signal." Ba quickly goes over the signals with me: four-seam, two-seam, curveball. Inside, outside. High, low. He taps his nose for pitches and points to different places on his face for location.

I go back to home plate, embarrassed at being called over *one minute* into the game. But Aaron and I do what Ba tells us to do, and the signals seem to work. Aaron throws six strikeouts in four innings.

One thing I notice about Aaron is that he loves going to full count. It doesn't make him nervous at all. Once the umpire calls three and two, Aaron gets this crazy little smile on his face and goes into his windup. A lot of times he comes out on top, too, maybe because the batters are getting weirded out about his smile.

"I like the battle," he tells me when I ask him about it. "From either side, as pitcher or batter. I like getting into tight spots, and fighting my way out. This is how you find out what you're made of."

Everyone on our team gets on base. *Everyone*. Not just Aaron, who works a triple out of a deep center field hit after getting drilled in the first inning, and Martin, who brings in two runs, but even Sean, who ekes out a base on balls. I get a double and two singles, no strikeouts. And Doug, *Doug*, taps a ball that drops softly between the shortstop and the outfield to give us the go-ahead run. His dad is waiting for him when he comes off the field.

"Are you kidding me, Dougie boy? A hit? An RBI?" Mr. Levinger picks Doug up in a big bear hug and then releases him. "Where'd you learn to hit like that?"

Doug points at Ba. "Coach. He made us do all these drills."

"When that ball went up, I asked my wife, 'What happened to Dougie's at bat?' And she said, 'No, Dougie hit that ball. *Dougie hit that ball.*'" *Dougie.* You had to feel for the guy.

"Da-ad," grumbles Doug. He drops his head and sits on the bench. "Quit it."

"You," says Mr. Levinger, grabbing Ba's hand and shaking it. "Are one *heck* of a coach."

Ba accepts the handshake awkwardly. "Douglas is a very hard worker," he says.

Mr. Levinger walks away, still shaking his head in amazement. "Great coach."

When we get home from the game, Laney comes running out of the living room, yelling, "Did you win? Did you win?"

I change my voice to sound like a sportscaster's. "At this point in the season, the Jaguars have a 100-percent winning record!"

Laney jumps around and cheers for us. Ba cocks his head at me. "It's 100 percent because the team has only played one game."

"I *know* that," I say. "But going one for one is still 100 percent!"

Ba shakes his head, but I think he is happy to win. He even stops by the living room and murmurs, "We won," to my mother before going upstairs to change.

Then it's my turn.

I take a deep breath, sit down next to Mom, and tell her all about the game. I tell her about Aaron throwing out the runner at first, and Doug's big hit. And she looks at me the whole time. In the eyes. And once, she says, "I bet that was exciting."

And then it's worth it, and the win feels real. The long, boring practices, the twenty swings every day. The forty fly balls and the forty grounders. I would have done a hundred, a thousand, just to get to this moment.

· CHAPTER ·
TWENTY-TWO

OF COURSE I HAD TOLD BA THAT I WOULD KEEP UP with my schoolwork when I started baseball. And at the time, I meant it. But the truth is, I let things get behind. I don't usually have that much homework, but sometimes, after practice, homework doesn't seem as important.

The easiest class to let things go in is history, Ms. Rowe. After I wrote two different reports about the election of 1912, it was like she felt guilty for giving me extra work. I get As on most of my work now, no matter how crummy it is. I got an A on my essay on the major outcomes of World War I, even though one of my points was that there was a decrease in the number of Austrian archdukes.

From there, it wasn't such a big leap to not turning in all of my work. But now, as Ms. Rowe is calling me up to her desk, I'm wondering if I've taken things too far.

"I'm missing your rough draft on an aspect of FDR's presidency," she says. "Did you turn it in?"

I am very tempted to lie. Ms. Rowe is known for losing papers, and it's only a rough draft, for Pete's sake. It's not a quiz or a test. She'll believe me.

But I don't. I don't want to lie to Ms. Rowe. I just want her to treat me like a regular kid.

"No," I say. "I did not."

"I see." She makes a note in her grade book, and her hair wavers a little bit as she does it. "Try to have it in by tomorrow, okay?" I nod and turn to go back to my seat when she calls me back.

"I also wanted to ask about a letter I sent to your parents," she says. "Did they have any questions?"

I look around the room for help. I'd put the letter far out of my mind. Chris glances up at that moment, and we look at each other for a split second before Chris looks away.

"My dad's kind of busy," I say. "He's coaching my baseball team."

"Your dad is coaching your baseball team?" Ms. Rowe's voice is loud enough for the whole class.

"Yes." I pitch my voice lower, hoping Ms. Rowe will follow.

"Hmm, well, I suppose that's good," says Ms. Rowe cautiously. "But you could still come to the group and rap with us."

"I'm busy, too," I tell her, backing away from her desk. Being around Ms. Rowe makes me feel twitchy.

On the way home, someone nudges my shoulder.

It's Chris.

He nudges me again. "Hey."

Chris and I used to walk home together all the time, from the time we were in kindergarten. Our moms used to wait at school and walk with us, and then, at some point, we were allowed to walk alone. I bet if you added it all up, it would be in the thousands, the number of times we've walked home. First days of school, last days, and rainy days. A couple of times, we walked back to school because one of us forgot something. Twice, we were sent home early from school because of snow.

None of those days, not a single one, does anything to make this moment less strange. We used to talk about a lot of stuff, but I can't think of any of those things right now. Because of the strike, we can't even talk about the Pirates. We used to spend hours talking about the games, players, opponents.

"Hi."

Chris draws a quick breath. "I heard your dad was coaching baseball."

"I think the whole class heard that."

Chris hiccups a quick laugh, a bit too loud. "Well, yeah. But that's something."

Chris knows, of course, how completely strange it is that Ba is coaching a baseball team. He has watched Ba say no to baseball over and over, usually after Chris asked if I could come out to play some ball. *No, Peter has homework. No, it's too late. No, Peter has chores.* Chris once told me that Ba was the only father he knew who seemed to actually *hate* baseball.

But still, I don't know what Chris means by *something*.

"Maybe you could come out tonight, play some ball with us," continues Chris. Hearing Chris say *us* startles me a bit. I was always on the other side of *us*.

"I have a game," I say.

"Then some other time," says Chris. "Anytime."

We're at my house now, at the walkway that leads to the front door, and beyond that, my mother is in a darkened room, with the light from the television flickering over her face. Chris, who my mother used to call her third son, knows nothing of this, I bet.

There was a time when I would not have dreamed of playing this game without Chris, but now he doesn't know why I'm playing, and I don't know how to tell him.

"Maybe," I tell him. But what I'm thinking is, probably not.

· CHAPTER ·
TWENTY-THREE

MARTIN PITCHES THE SECOND GAME.

"You might want to put some extra padding in your glove," he cracks. "You've got a real pitcher today." Martin only throws fastballs, four seam and two seam, but he throws with a lot of power and control. I barely have to move my glove. If I didn't want to win this game, I swear I'd drop his pitches and move my glove out of the strike zone just to take him down a peg.

At first, Martin gets the strikeouts against the other team, the Falcons. He knows that a high, inside fastball is downright irresistible. He also plants a few on just the outside that send the batters chasing after the ball, making them look like they're trying to catch butterflies.

In spite of a good start, though, some of the better players start getting hits off Martin when they get up to bat a second time. By the end of the third inning, it's 5–4, Falcons.

At the top of the fourth, it's bases loaded, but Martin

151

has worked the count to 0–2. Then I hear a voice behind me and rustling behind the backstop. And then there's a smell, sour and old.

"Boy. Ya gotta step into it." The voice stops for a moment, and there's a deep breath. Then the smell gets stronger.

I peer around the umpire and see a man dressed in a button-down shirt and dark blue pants. I've never seen him before, but he must be Martin's dad.

Martin acts like he can't hear his father. He goes into his windup and fires one in. It's a little outside, and the ump calls a ball.

"A ball? Are you kidding me? Are you blind?" Mr. Greer hisses to the umpire. Then he raises his voice. "You get him out, ya hear me? Don't walk this kid."

The umpire turns slightly, so more of his back is toward Martin's father. But it doesn't make Mr. Greer go away. I lower my head, silently grateful Mom isn't here today. This is the last thing I'd want her to see, the ugliness and stench.

Ba signals for a curveball. I have to lunge to the side to get the ball. Martin is down, 2–2 in the count.

Martin has an expression I haven't seen before. I see his chin wobbling right before he puts his glove up in front of his face. One eye stares out and blinks.

"*You strike him out!*" roars Mr. Greer.

Ba signals for a four-seam fastball, Martin's most reliable pitch. Martin goes into his windup and throws the ace. In a split second, I see the ball is not coming in on target—it hits the batter square in the hip.

"Ugh!" The batter drops his bat and falls to the ground. I jump back and look down at him. His eyes squeeze shut in pain.

The Falcons coach comes out and checks on the batter. After a minute, the kid gets up and limps to first base, rubbing his hip while the parents clap politely.

"Yeah, you rub it, you big baby," says Mr. Greer. "A real player shows no pain." He raises his voice. "You showed him, didn't ya!" The runner on third comes home, touches the base with his toe, and darts away. No one wants to be around Mr. Greer.

"Now listen here," starts the umpire.

"Bend your back!" shouts Mr. Greer. "And let's see some strikeouts!"

The umpire turns to face Mr. Greer. "I can have you thrown out!"

"Don't tell me what to do!" says Mr. Greer.

"You must be Mr. Greer." In the middle of Mr. Greer's sizzling anger comes another voice.

It is Ba.

"I am so pleased you could come to a game," says Ba.

My father's comments are enough to distract Mr. Greer. He whips his head away from the umpire and looks at my dad, slightly confused.

"It is so hot out here, in the sun," my father continues. His voice is dry and smooth as a stone, the one he uses with the neighbors and customers at the pharmacy. "I know that Martin pitches so well because of you, but perhaps you would be more comfortable in the dugout?"

Mr. Greer stares blankly at my father for a second, as if suddenly remembering where he is. "No," he says, turning abruptly. "I'm done here. I just came to see the kid pitch for a while." He swings around to go, and the turn unsteadies him. He walks unevenly out to the parking lot.

No one says anything when Mr. Greer walks away, but I can feel a shift in the crowd, among the players, like a breeze on a summer day. Relief. Ba calls a time-out, and signals the infield to come to the mound.

As Ba and I walk toward him, Martin narrows his eyes at us and folds his arms across his chest. All the other kids come running in.

"What was going *on* out there?" asks Jimmy. "Was that your dad, Martin?" He gives Martin a puzzled, wide-eyed look.

Martin looks at Jimmy dead-on. "I have no idea who that was," he says. "Some old drunk, I guess."

"Wow," says Jimmy, giggling a little. "Crazy old guy."

I struggle to keep my mouth from falling open. I had heard Ba say, "You must be Martin's father," and the man had not denied it, but I guess I was the only one close enough to hear. I study Ba's face, checking for some sign of disapproval. But Ba does not correct Martin.

"You must be careful around strangers," he says.

Martin lifts his chin at Ba. "I suppose you're pulling me out of the game."

"Being able to pitch at all under those conditions is a sign of a very good pitcher," says Ba. "It reminded me of Branch Rickey testing Jackie Robinson's ability to handle hostile crowds before he signed him."

Aaron shakes his head. "I couldn't pitch with someone yelling at me."

Rickey puffs out his chest. "See? You can always count on someone named Rickey to be cool." All of the other players laugh at Rickey's joke, except Martin. He turns his head; his hands open and close.

"You are doing just fine, Martin," says Ba. "I am sure that the team would be very appreciative if you stayed in."

Martin glances at the rest of the team and shrugs. "I

can do that," says Martin, as if he's doing us all a huge favor.

"C'mon, everyone, buck up," says Aaron. "It's called a game 'cause it's supposed to be *fun*."

We end up losing by three runs. No surprise there. And maybe it's no surprise that no one is there to pick up Martin. Martin, Ba, and I lean against our car, watching the last of the team leave.

"That umpire, he was calling a tight strike zone," complains Martin. He wants to act like it's not his fault.

"It's part of the game," says Ba. "The other team had the same strike zone." He reaches over and unlocks the driver's-side door. "We should go. Get in, Martin. I will give you a ride home."

Martin shifts. "Nah," he says. "It's all right. Go on. My mom will be here any minute."

I'm tired. And hungry. I open the door on the passenger side. "Okay, so let's go."

Ba shakes his head. "That would not be responsible. We can wait."

Martin scans the road, looking east and west. Finally, after a few more minutes, he says, "I guess it would be okay for you to drive me home."

"Good," says Ba. Then to me, "Sit in the back with Martin."

Martin and I sit in the back of the car, not speaking. I watch the landscape change out the window. Martin directs Ba to the edge of town, where there are more trees and the stores are more spread out.

"Stop here," Martin suddenly announces. I hate the way Martin speaks to my father, like my father is his driver, his servant. And Ba just takes it.

Ba slows the car. "Here?" he asks. There is no house, not as far as we can see. There is a dirt road going off to the right from the main road, leading into the woods.

"This is fine," says Martin.

"Where is your house?" asks Ba. The car still rolls, slowly.

Martin waves vaguely at the dirt road. "It's down there. You don't need to drive down there."

The car picks up speed. "I will take you there," says Ba. "I will feel better if I see you go in your house."

Martin sighs noisily and rolls his eyes. As we drive into the woods, I see a row of not-very-nice-looking houses. They have weedy front yards, broken screen doors, and curtains drooping in the windows. Martin tells my father that his house is the fifth one on the right. It's a one-story house; the wooden siding needs painting and the chimney is crumbling.

Martin sits in the car for a moment. Then he grabs his glove. "Well, bye," he says to Ba.

"Good job today, Martin," says Ba.

Martin heads straight into the house; he doesn't look back at our car once. After the screen door slams behind him, a face looks out. It is the man from the game.

"I knew it," I say from the backseat.

"Keep your opinions to yourself," Ba says sharply.

"What? About what?"

Ba bobs his head to indicate the ribbon of road disappearing behind us. "About Martin. His father. Where he lives."

"So you knew! Why didn't you say anything?"

"It is none of my business," says Ba calmly.

I feel like my head is going to explode. This kindness, this courtesy that my father extends to Martin is beyond my comprehension.

"Why are you doing this?" I ask.

"Driving Martin home?" asks Ba. He seems genuinely confused.

"Why are you protecting him? And why did you act

like he was doing us a huge favor by continuing to pitch?" I'm so mad it feels like the words are shooting out of my mouth like bullets. And I can't even bring myself to say what I really want to say. *Do you know what he says about you behind your back?*

"We *did* need a pitcher," says Ba. "Aaron was not ready to pitch again, and I think Jimmy is not quite ready to pitch." He gives me a significant look. "No one else on the team can or will pitch."

So that's what this is about. He's still mad about me not pitching. For *defying* him.

"You're the one who always says to tell the truth," I say, half under my breath.

"And you're old enough to know the difference between a lie to save yourself, and a lie to . . ." Ba hesitates. "An omission to be kind."

"Kindness? For Martin?" I say. "You're the coach; he should just do what you tell him. You shouldn't have to suck up to him." I slouch down in my seat. "I just wish you had let him feel lousy for a while, cause that's how he makes everyone else feel."

Ba is silent for a moment, and then he asks, "Is that what I should do? Act out of vengeance and spite?"

I slink lower into my seat. "I'm just saying, maybe he should know how other people feel," I mumble.

"How can Martin learn the correct way to behave if I do not show him?" asks Ba.

I don't answer Ba. Some people talk about signals getting crossed, but our words just whiz by each other, never intersecting. They are parallel lines that never make contact.

If Ba and I are trading words that don't connect, then Mom is just a black hole where my words disappear.

"Mom, I got a double today. I got stranded, but it was a nice hit, right down the third-base line." I am grateful she did not come to today's game so I can only tell her the good parts.

Nothing.

"I had some good catches, too. Martin had a wild pitch that I had to jump up and catch!" I crouch down on the floor and leap up into the air to show her.

Her eyes never move from the television screen. I look over at the TV to see what is so interesting. It's a commercial for a supermarket. I'm not as interesting as new cash registers or double coupons.

A cold, dizzy feeling sweeps over me. *Why isn't this working? What am I doing wrong?*

From where I am, kneeling on the floor, I look at Mom, look at her expression. Her eyes remind me of the goldfish we see in Chinese restaurants—dark and expressionless. No one knows what they are seeing or thinking, either.

I swallow hard and force myself to push away Martin and the lost game. I will not give up.

I start to tell her about a game, a different game. A game she can't ignore. The best game ever played.

I start at the bottom of the third, when we were down 5–4. But now, instead of Martin's dad showing up, I have Martin pitching the game of his life. Going to full count and getting the strikeout. Fiery fastballs and mind-boggling curveballs. It's killing me to say these things, but it's the best I can make up on the fly. I have to let the rest of the team get some credit, too, so Rickey turns a line drive into a double play, second to first.

Mom keeps looking at the TV, but I won't stop talking. I have our batters struggle against mighty odds—a bad call and a lucky catch. Then I figure Coop won't mind if I turn his base on balls into a sweet hit on an 0–2 pitch. And I give myself a steal to second base.

I do insert some truthful things—like the way Aaron always taps the bat three times before settling into his stance and the way you can tell Jimmy and Bobby apart by the way they run the bases. I tell her about how Rickey puffs out his chest after he gets a hit, and how Sean never swings on the first pitch. But as for the rest, it's a great game that anyone would want to play in—the come-from-behind victory, great plays. I decide not to give myself credit for the game-winning hit. I figure Aaron might like that honor.

By the time I am done, I almost believe my own story. I *want* to believe my own story; I want to be on that team.

Finally, Mom speaks.

"That is something." She glances at me when she says that. She might even be talking about something on TV, like a knife that can cut through a metal can, or glue that can hold a construction worker from a beam, but it's something. I'll take it.

"What part?" I ask, trying to lure her closer to me, just for a moment. "What part did you like the best?"

She is quiet for a moment. Then she says, "Your steal to second."

For a moment, her words sear me, because maybe if I really had had a steal, she would feel even better about it. The next game will be better, I vow. Truly.

As I get up to leave, I realize that my father is standing in the hallway, right outside the living room. My heart speeds up. I do not know how long he has been listening.

I walk by him, waiting for him to say something. But he doesn't. He lets me walk away without a word, but I'm not sure what I'm getting away with. Maybe I am getting a pass because we are both liars today, trying to convince ourselves that the situation is not so bad.

·CHAPTER·
TWENTY-FOUR

I DON'T KNOW HOW AARON FIGURED OUT WHERE WE live, but he's here, after dinner, asking if I want to go down to Folger's Lot.

"Haven't you had enough baseball today?" I ask. Aaron is still in his uniform, and has a huge smile on his face, like we didn't just get creamed earlier in the day.

"C'mon, it'll be fun," says Aaron.

"I'm kinda sore," I say.

"We'll play easy," says Aaron. "It's just for fun."

I wonder if Chris will be there. "I think it might rain."

Aaron snorts. "You never played in the rain before?"

"Hello, Aaron," says Ba, who has come to see who is at the front door. "Did you need something?"

After Aaron tells Ba why he's there, I expect Ba to tell Aaron no, because I have homework or I have chores to do. But instead, Ba reaches over and pushes the screen door open wider.

"Get your glove," he tells me. "And come home when the street lights come on."

Aaron and I walk over to Sean's house, and then the three of us walk down to the lot. There's no one else there.

"People are probably still eating," says Sean, who skipped dessert to come out with us.

Aaron finds a brown paper grocery bag, folds it up, and puts a rock on top to make first base. A flattened RC Cola can is designated as second, and we pile weeds into a mound for third. Aaron hits first, I pitch, and Sean fields.

I throw an easy, swooping pitch and Aaron gives it a nice knock into shallow left. The rule is that the runner has to stop once the pitcher gets the ball again. Aaron gets a double.

"Ghost runner," announces Aaron, heading back to home.

Aaron gets a single on his next at bat, which puts the ghost runner at third. The ghost runner moves up as many bases as the runner.

"One more to score," announces Aaron, picking up his bat and giving it a very confident twirl in the air.

"You wish," I say. I try to get him with an outside pitch, but Aaron lays his bat on it. Sean darts over and scoops up the ball right before it hits the ground.

"Nice one," I call. Since he made the out, Sean gets to bat next, I move into the field, and Aaron pitches.

Sean whiffs the first two pitches. He starts turning red. He hasn't had a hit yet in a game, which I'm sure is bugging him.

Aaron starts to wind up, and then stops. "You're all right," says Aaron. "You can do this." His voice is quiet and encouraging. "Open your stance a little."

Sean moves his feet uncertainly. Aaron throws a soft pitch and Sean tightens his grip and swings hard. *Unnngh!* It's a lot of effort, for absolutely no payoff, not even a tip.

Sean shakes his head in disgust, finds the ball, and sidearms it back to Aaron. Then he holds out the bat to me.

My turn goes on for a while. If Sean can't hit for love or money, then it's like I can't *not* hit. I swing at everything—tomahawk swings at pitches that are practically over my head, golf swings near the ground, and everything in between. The bat and ball keep connecting and sending the ball out into the field. Me and the ghost runner, we go around and around. Three runs, four runs, five runs.

After the fifth run, Aaron throws his head back and laughs. "Aren't you tired?"

"Maybe the ghost runner," I say. "Not me."

"I thought you were sore," says Aaron, reminding me of my comment earlier. I'd forgotten the excuse I'd first made up.

"That game today," I start. "Lousy, huh?"

"You can say that again," says Sean. He's standing on the mound, contemplating his next pitch. "That guy showing up. He really got to Martin."

"C'mon," I hear myself say. "That wasn't a stranger showing up. That was Martin's dad." I ignore the little voice in my head, reminding me that Ba told me to keep my mouth shut.

"Really?" says Sean, his eyes growing wide.

"I figured," says Aaron. "That explains a lot, doesn't it?"

"Yeah," I say. "It does."

"But, even without Martin's dad, it just wasn't our game," says Aaron. "Everyone has games like that, even the majors, where the team just can't get it right. The best hitter can't hit, the first baseman can't get the out. The pitcher's a mess. It happens. Ya gotta shake it off."

"Shake it off? What if your team is just flat-out bad?" I ask.

Aaron cocks his head to one side. "Do you really think our team is bad?"

I try to think about our team as honestly as I can. We have good players, bad players, and in-between players. "I don't know," I say.

"Look at it this way," says Aaron. "Part of the game is up here." He points to his temple. "Like with a batting slump? It's not that the batter is not able to hit the ball; it's that he thinks he can't hit the ball."

I try not to look at Sean when Aaron says this, but I'm pretty sure I can hear him sigh. If anyone's in a slump, it's Sean.

Aaron continues, "It's the same with the team. You think your team is bad, you have a bad game, and then you think it's because the team is bad and you don't bother trying. You think your team is good and just having a bad day? Then you can come back from that. See?"

More kids start showing up as Sean finally catches the out that ends my turn. I'm thinking that we'll just start playing with bigger teams, but instead, Aaron has a different idea.

"Let's play Pepper."

In Pepper, one person is the hitter and everyone else is a fielder and pitcher. The batter hits the ball, and whoever fields the ball pitches it back so that the batter is "peppered" with pitches from all directions.

The fielders line up, and one of the new kids goes first, a fourth grader named Tommy. He hits about a dozen balls before Aaron catches a line drive and Tommy's turn is over. By the rules, it's now Aaron's turn. On his first at bat, he hits one aloft, almost directly to Sean. Sean barely has to move his glove to catch it.

"You're out," says a kid who goes by Bucky, probably because he has two large front teeth that stick out under his top lip. "It's his turn." He points at Sean.

Aaron shoulders the bat. "That was a short turn," he says. "Can we say that everyone gets at least three hits?"

Bucky thinks it over; apparently, he's the unofficial chief of the new kids who have shown up. "From now on," says Bucky. "Not starting with you. That wouldn't be fair."

Aaron gives in immediately, which surprises me, since Bucky is younger than us. "Okay," Aaron says. He hands the bat over to Sean. "Three-hit minimum, starting with Sean."

We return to the fielding line. Before Sean can get settled into his stance, Aaron yells, "Pepper!" and launches the ball toward Sean.

Sean barely has time to react. He turns his head

toward the ball and jerks back, and then awkwardly swings the bat. There's a soft *thunk* as the bat and ball connect, and the ball rolls toward Tommy.

Tommy immediately grabs the ball and pitches it back. "Pepper!"

This time, Sean is just a hair more settled in his stance. He pops the ball back, dropping it just behind the line. It's closest to me and I scramble to get it.

"Hurry!" whispers Aaron. "Before Sean has time to think."

So this is what Aaron is up to; he is trying to get Sean to hit before he has time to think about it, or psych himself out. My pitch is a little bit on the outside, but Sean adjusts by taking a step forward and swinging. A line drive cuts through the middle of our group.

"No one's getting that one!" shouts Aaron.

We go around and around, playing Pepper, then Three Flies Up, then Over the Line. We change sides and positions, borrow gloves, and change the rules as we go along. Tommy gets to take two steps closer to the line for Over the Line because he's the youngest. It's my turn to try to hit the ball through the other side when a figure, just beyond the edge of the lot near the trees, catches my eye.

At first it's barely a shadow, but as it moves out of the trees, I can see it more clearly. Slender in build, longish dark hair. He has his hands in the pockets of his jean jacket and he's looking directly at our game, as if to see what all the noise is about.

I could swear it's Nelson.

Somewhere behind me, someone is calling my name, but I'm just trying to look more closely at this person. The man's face is harder to see, especially when the breeze pushes his hair across it. But the jean jacket. The way he stands.

My pulse is thundering through my veins. I feel hot and cold at the same time. I take a few steps closer. *Could it be?*

Suddenly, I'm jerked backward roughly. Someone is holding me at the elbow.

It's Ba. "Didn't you hear me calling you?"

In that split second, I lose sight of the man. When I look back, he's gone. The other boys are now gathered together, staring at me and Ba.

"How long have you been here?" I ask, wondering if Ba saw what I saw.

"A few minutes. I came to look for you," says Ba. He points at the streetlights, glowing against the rapidly darkening sky. "You were supposed to be home fifteen minutes ago." He turns to the other boys. "I suspect you all were supposed to be home by now."

He didn't see. He never sees what I see.

"Are you okay?" asks Aaron.

"Throw away the trash," says Ba, pointing to our bases.

I'm not going to say what I saw, or what I thought I saw. It makes no sense. They might think I've gone crazy, or worse, Ba will give me ten reasons why I'm wrong, and I don't want to be wrong.

"I thought I saw someone I knew," I tell Aaron.

Ghost runner.

· CHAPTER ·
TWENTY-FIVE

Eagles fly high
Eagles fly low
Eagles get hits
And home runs you know.

THE PARENTS ON THE OTHER TEAM END THEIR CHANT by flapping their arms and yelling, "Gooooo Eagles!" I hate them. I hate the way they sit and talk to each other. I hate the way they laugh after they chant, like they know it's silly, but they can't help themselves.

But most of all, I hate them because it's working. We are down 10–2.

Bobby and I stare at the Eagles parents. "I wish they would shut up already," says Bobby. His dad is here, but he is not the cheering type. There seem to be more parents at the game than usual; I think it's because of the strike. People are getting desperate for baseball.

We should be able to beat these guys, but it's the top of the fourth and we are falling apart. We just can't make the outs, even the easy ones. Rickey misses a soft pop-up. Jimmy overthrows to first. Yonder loses a ball along the fence line. The Eagles scored seven runs in this inning before we could get that last, miserable third out.

The team jogs to the dugout, not so much because anyone is in a hurry to bat, but because they just want to leave the field. Before anyone can put on a batting helmet, though, Ba comes into the dugout, looking worried.

"The umpire just told me that he will call the slaughter rule if the game gets much worse," says Ba.

"Don't worry," said Aaron. "We're going to close the gap this inning." The slaughter rule says that if one team is down more than ten runs by the end of the fourth inning, the ump can declare the game over.

I pace up and down the dugout, wishing for a comeback. I imagine telling Mom, "We were down eight runs, the ump was threatening to call the slaughter rule, and then we came back!" I slip my fingers through the chain-link fence at the front of the dugout, squeezing with all my might.

But it doesn't look so good. Jimmy pops out, and then Bobby strikes out swinging, giving us two quick outs.

That gets us down to our two worst hitters, Doug and Yonder. Doug hits a dribbler back to the pitcher that rightfully should be an out, but mercifully, the pitcher overthrows to first and Doug makes it safely on base.

Yonder, who usually hits the ball straight into someone's glove, tees off four foul balls before he gets a sharply hit single down the third-base line. Doug makes it to second easily. Against all odds, we have two men on.

The team gets on its feet. We are at the most reliable part of our lineup now, Aaron, and then Martin. They almost always get on base. I stare at the back of Aaron's shirt, trying to will him to get a hit that will bring home Yonder.

"Two-out ral-ly!" It's Sean, Rickey, and me, trying to get the rest of the team going. Our words sound sad instead of encouraging, but we persist.

Out of the corner of my eye, I see Ba give the signal. He sweeps his right hand over his left arm, and then tugs on his wrist. *Take.*

Take? I don't believe it. Why would Ba call for a take? I look to Aaron for his reaction, but he just nods. He takes his time walking to home plate. He stops to tap the dirt off his cleats and adjusts his shirt.

The pitcher pulls his cap down low, studying Aaron for a moment. Then he goes into his windup.

The pitch is a beaut, straight and fast. Aaron watches it go by.

Aaron looks back at Ba. This time, he stacks his fists and points at Aaron. *Swing away*.

The next pitch is outside. Then Aaron watches a pitch go by, which the ump calls a strike. 1–2. The dugout groans at the call. "Looked like a ball to me," I say to no one in particular.

The next pitch is low. Ball two. The next one is in the dirt. Ball three. Full count.

Sean and I holler as loud as we can: "That's too low! That's too low! That is where the wormies go!"

I think about what Aaron said about going to full count, about finding out what you're made of, and hope he is made of something really good inside today. A double, anyway.

The pitcher shakes off the first signal, then nods, and goes into his windup.

I can't watch and I have to watch. *C'mon, Aaron!* This is the best and worst part of baseball, to put so much hope on hitting a small, fast-moving ball with a two-inch-wide stick.

Aaron swings. It's a beautiful swing—tight and quick. But it's no good.

"Hunh," calls the umpire, drawing back his arm.

Disappointment takes an extra moment to set in because it happens so quickly.

The other team scores four runs in the next inning. Our fight is gone. They don't even have any outs when the ump declares the game over.

The mood in the dugout is dark. This ending doesn't feel merciful, which is the other name for the slaughter rule. The mercy rule. It feels humiliating. We watch the other team walk happily to their cars. I hear one of them say they are going for ice cream. I wonder what I am going to tell Mom.

Martin comes over and pokes Aaron in the shoulder, hard. "You know why they call it a game? 'Cause there are winners and losers."

Sean takes a few steps toward them. "Hey." He holds up his hands. "There's no telling what would have happened, even if Aaron had gotten a hit."

Martin shakes his head. "Yeah, but I don't want this to happen again, you know? And we need to talk about this so it won't happen again." From the way Martin curls his hands, I'm not sure he is necessarily interested in *talking*.

Aaron covers his head with his hands. "I know, I know. I'm a sucker for the high fastball, okay?"

"Maybe you're just a sucker in general," says Martin. He raises his voice. "Maybe we're all suckers, thinking that we could win with this chop suey coach of ours." He spits on the dugout floor. "Telling you to *take* on the first pitch."

The fact that I agree with Martin makes this all the more painful.

"That pitch was a *gift*." He glares at Aaron. "You shouldn't have listened to him."

"He's the coach," says Aaron.

"He shouldn't be." The silence in the dugout suggests that, at best, this point is debatable.

"Yeah, well, you're so busy complaining about Mr. Lee, but when that guy asked for volunteers to coach, he's the only one that offered," says Sean.

"And your dad wasn't available, right, Martin?" says Aaron quietly.

Martin lets out a howl and lunges for Aaron, pinning him to the chain-link side of the dugout. Sean grabs Martin from behind. "Knock it off! Knock it off!" Sean yells. Jimmy and Bobby jam themselves in between Martin and Aaron.

"You do not talk about my dad!" screams Martin. "Don't ever talk about my dad." Even with Sean holding him from behind, Martin breaks free enough to pull back his fist.

I stick out my hand to block his punch. "Stop it!" If Ba finds out that I talked about Martin's dad, I'm in trouble. "Knock it off!"

"Let him!" hollers Aaron. "And that will be last punch he throws."

Martin's eyes get wide and he drops his fist. He takes a step back, staring at Aaron as if he's turned into a snake.

"You . . . you . . ." That is all Martin can say.

I turn around to look at Aaron.

The first thing I think of is a tail. Something that doesn't belong. But it's one long braid hanging out of Aaron's baseball cap.

"You're a girl," says Martin. His voice rises and squeaks. A *girl*?

• CHAPTER •
TWENTY-SIX

THERE ARE RULES EVERYONE KNOWS AND THERE ARE rules everyone has to figure out for themselves. Everyone knows that girls aren't supposed to play baseball.

"You're a girl," says Martin. "Now I've seen everything."

I'm too stunned to speak. I can only look. Aaron, star baseball player, has suddenly turned into a girl. Without the cap, long brown hair falls into her eyes. She pushes herself into the chain-link fence because that is the only place she can go. We surround her, our loss suddenly forgotten.

"How long have you been a girl?" asks Jimmy.

Aaron narrows her eyes at him. "How long do you think?"

"You lied to us," says Rickey.

"I never said I was a boy." She folds her arms in front of her and stares at us.

"What's your real name?" asks Sean.

"It's Aaron," she says. "You know that."

"No, your *real* name," says Doug.

"I told you. It's Erin. E-R-I-N." She spells her name as if we should have known all along. Like it's our fault.

"You let us think it was Aaron, like Hank Aaron. I saw your name on the roster," I say. I say this like the force of this argument will make Aaron change back into a boy. But no, I had told a *girl* about Nelson.

"Let's just say that I let everyone make their own assumptions," says Erin. "People see what they expect to see."

That is definitely true. With all that time we spent together, I never guessed, but with the cap off, I can't believe I didn't see it earlier. The name. The slightly high-pitched voice. And, now that I look more carefully, a not-quite-right body shape.

"Letting people spell your name wrong—that's cheating," says Rickey.

"No one asked me how to spell my name," says Erin. "Did you spell your name when you registered?" She lifts her chin slightly.

Martin points at her. "You took a cup, an athletic cup. You wouldn't have taken one if you weren't trying to fool us."

Leave it to Martin to find the most incriminating evidence.

For the first time, Erin's bravery falters. Her chin drops. "I was supposed to take one," she says. "It was part of the uniform."

"You wearing it now?" asks Bobby. "Show us."

"That's how you found Nelson's bat," I say, putting it all together. "You were using the latrine." Erin nods her head, ever so slightly, but does not look at me.

"Teammates don't lie to each other," says Coop.

Erin spreads her hands open wide, pleading. "Look, I just wanted to play ball. On a team. That's all. Isn't that what we all want to do?" She pushes her hair off her face. "Everything I did, I did as me, Erin."

A few guys nod their heads, but don't say anything. All I can think of is Aaron giving me Nelson's bat back. Erin.

Rickey's mom walks into the dugout. As soon as she sees Erin, her eyes get big. "What's going on here? Who is that?"

"It's Aaron," says Rickey. "He's a girl."

"Oh my goodness," says Rickey's mom, pulling him toward her so that her arm is a shield around him. "Rickey, you've been playing with *a girl*?"

Ba walks into the dugout. He glances at us, his eyes widening slightly when he sees Erin. But the only thing he says is, "We need to clear out the dugout for the next game."

"Did you know about this?" accuses Rickey's mom. Rickey shakes his head and covers his eyes.

More parents come into the dugout. Their voices snake around us, surprised and accusing, all at the same time.

"Is this the one who struck out with two men on? No wonder we lost."

"It's just unnatural, girls playing sports."

"A girl, huh? Probably put here by some women's libbers. Well, I'm sure the coach will have something to say about that!"

He doesn't.

With each comment, Erin seems to get smaller and smaller. Some parents don't even say anything. They just walk in, stare at Erin, and leave. Erin finally puts her cap back on, which makes it all seem a little less awful.

Erin's dad walks in, the score book tucked under his arm. He just says, "Let's go," and Erin walks out behind him. "I told you this would happen," I hear him say in a low voice.

"I just wanted to play," says Erin.

When she walks by me, her glove brushes against mine. Erin gives me a pleading look. I can almost hear her whisper in my ear. *It's called a game because it's supposed to be fun.*

Ba quietly picks up the bats and balls and puts them into the equipment bag, and hands me a paper bag to put the trash in. I can hear the other parents whispering and looking at Ba.

Doug's dad walks up to the rear of the dugout, and rests his arms on the sloped roof. "Mr. Lee," he says. "What are you going to do about this?"

Ba holds his hand up and nods his head as if to say, *Yes, I hear you.* But he doesn't say anything else.

I think that another coach would handle this right away. Another coach would take charge and say to everyone, "Okay, folks, here's what we're going to do," and everyone would nod and listen to him. But not my father; he is not that kind of man. He is not a *heckuva game* kind of dad. My father is the kind of man who lets the rottenest kid on the team save face. The kind who picks the slowest kid in the league as his special pick for the team. He bows his head away from the other parents as he finishes cleaning up the dugout and lets the team scatter, with bad feelings and confusion.

He is silent, and for the moment, even with all these thoughts inside me, so am I. And I do not know who I hate more for it.

·CHAPTER·
TWENTY-SEVEN

THE FIRST THING I DO WHEN WE GET HOME IS GO TO the living room to be with Mom. I just want to be with her, to have whatever little comfort there is in being next to her. I want to pretend for a few minutes that Aaron is still a boy.

"Mom?"

She doesn't move from her spot on the couch; she is lying down and her back is to me, so I walk around to get a better angle. I watch for her chest to rise and fall under the blankets. There is no movement.

A very terrible thought enters my head.

What is the least amount of effort you need to live? What's the smallest amount you can eat, how many breaths do you need, what's the tiniest bit of caring you need to give and receive to hold fast in the world? What happens when that little bit disappears?

I take a step closer and force myself to raise my voice. "Mom?" I blink hard.

Suddenly Mom rolls to one side. "Peter."

At the sound of her voice, my body goes weak. I lower myself to the floor, so our faces are at the same level. I get so close to her face that I see each individual eyelash and the tiny freckles across her cheeks. It's all I can do not to reach out and hold on to her with all my might. "We're home," I say. I hope I sound normal, like after any game.

She nods and closes her eyes.

The phone begins to ring. Ba answers the phone calls, and most of the time, it seems like the other person is doing most of the talking. Ba says things like, "I see," and, "I appreciate that you have brought this to my attention." He stands near the phone on the kitchen wall, letting the cord curl and twist. After the third phone call, I ask him who is calling, though I have a pretty good idea.

Ba sighs and rubs his forehead with his fingers. "The first two phone calls were from Mr. Lattimore, Jimmy and Bobby's father, and Mr. Cooper, Danny's father."

"What did they say?"

"Mr. Lattimore and Mr. Cooper explained to me that they do not want their sons to attend practice or play in games until Erin is off the team."

"They can do that?" I ask. "Just up and leave the team? You're not going to let that happen, are you? We're going to keep playing, aren't we?"

I can't think of what will happen if the team falls apart, if there are no more games. The team needs more time to play. Mom hasn't gone to a game yet.

Ba waits a moment before speaking. "The third phone call was from Mr. Nickelson," he says, finally. "He said he would understand if I wanted Erin to leave the team." Then he adds, "But I do not think she should leave the team."

"You don't?" My father has been so quiet that I am surprised he actually has an opinion.

"No," says Ba. "Erin is a good player. She has not done anything to deserve getting kicked off the team."

"Three guys could leave the team if you let her play. She's just one player."

"That is true," says Ba. "But there is also a question of fairness. Is it fair to take Erin off the team?"

Ba crosses his arms and looks down, as if the answer is in the folds of his arms. "Some of those parents, they said if I let Erin play, I'm a 'women libber.'" He says the strange words slowly. I guess he means women's libber.

I think back to the conversation Mom and I had

about the Equal Rights Amendment. Mom could be a women's libber, too. Then again, she's supposed to be a lot of things right now that she's not.

Ba shrugs. "I don't think I am a women libber, but maybe I am. Should Elaine not be allowed to do something because she's a girl?" I think of Elaine. Sure, she's a pest and a pain, and there are some things she can't do because she's still little, but if someone treated Elaine the way some of the parents treated Erin today? Made her feel the way Erin looked when she left?

My heart feels like a lion's. But then I think of that terrible moment when we got home, and fear washes over me, extinguishing everything else.

"We have to keep playing." I say.

Ba rubs his scalp, and I realize that my father's hair is turning white. It has been pure black for as long as I've been alive.

"Some things are more important than baseball," says Ba. "You just want to keep playing baseball."

His comment fills me with bitterness.

"If the season ends early, you'll probably be glad to be done coaching." I say. "All that extra work. You can go back to the way things were."

Ba looks away for a moment. "I have always been prepared to complete this season," he says.

"If Erin stays on the team, and the team breaks up, then what's the point?" I ask. "Nothing changes."

"Sometimes you just have to know that you have done what is right. You cannot control the outcome, only your own actions," says Ba.

"I want to keep playing," I say stubbornly.

Ba looks down, studying the wood floor. "There must be another way, then."

But I don't see how. I don't see how Erin can play and still have the team play. I feel the way I did with the division with decimals problems. The answers seemed to jump away from me any time I got close. Until Nelson explained it, anyway. For what seems like the millionth time, I wish that Nelson were here to tell me what to do, to help me figure this out.

· CHAPTER ·
TWENTY-EIGHT

"HAS YOUR DAD DECIDED? ABOUT ERIN, I MEAN," asks Sean.

I shake my head. "He wants her to stay on the team. But it's complicated."

Sean and me, we're sitting on the concrete step outside the kitchen door. Sean said he came over to play catch, but clearly, he really wants to talk about Erin.

"She shouldn't have lied," says Sean.

"Well, yeah, but she wouldn't have gotten to play if she told the truth." This is the hard part. As much as I try to just think about my mom, I keep thinking about Erin, too.

"My dad says that it's not safe for girls to play sports," says Sean. "They get hurt more easily. They'll ruin the game for the rest of us."

"Erin never got hurt more than anyone else," I say. "And when she did, she didn't make a big deal out of it."

"Hmmm," says Sean. "Well, maybe she really wanted to cry, but she was afraid we'd find out she was a girl."

"But she didn't cry. That's the point."

Sean scratches his knee. "It's not normal," says Sean. "Girls playing baseball."

I think about my family. I used to think of us as normal, in a Mom, Dad, and three kids sort of way. Not anymore, though.

"There is a difference between being *wrong* and *not normal*," I say. "Normal just means like everyone else. A long time ago, cars weren't normal because not everyone had one. Not being normal doesn't mean *bad*."

Sean nods, but he doesn't say whether he thinks I'm wrong or right. The thing about Erin is, she treated me the same after finding out about Nelson; she didn't give me the silent treatment or try to treat me extra special. And that counts for something in my book.

"And you," I say, testing him. "You want her kicked off the team."

"I didn't say that. I said it wasn't normal, that's all. You gotta admit, we'd get some funny looks from the other teams."

"Yeah, okay. But maybe they wouldn't have to know." I lower my voice, even though it's just the two of us. "The thing is, some of the parents on our team are saying they'll pull their kids off the team if Erin stays. If enough parents do it, we won't have a team anymore."

"You had to figure that would happen," says Sean.

I hadn't figured. "So, what about you? Would you leave the team if Erin stays?"

Sean looks surprised. "If you're still on the team, then I am, too. What kind of person just takes off and leaves a friend behind?" He says this like it's common sense. A lot of what's common sense to Sean is hard for other people; it's what I like about him. I think back to the day I complained when Ba picked Sean for the team with his free pick. Sean, with his chug-chug running and slow hands. My cheeks warm with shame.

I used to think Chris left me behind. Now I'm wondering whether I share the blame. Maybe Chris didn't leave me behind; maybe I didn't give him much to hold on to, either.

"And don't forget, my dad's so excited I'm playing a sport, he won't pull me off," says Sean. He finds a tiny pebble and wings it into the backyard. And another one. And another one.

"He'll complain, but that's about it," continues Sean. "What's really bugging my dad is that a girl is a better player than me."

"You're not a bad player," I say.

Sean shakes his head. "Dad actually used to talk about Erin, back when she was a boy." He deepens his voice, imitating Mr. Tyrell. *"Did you see how Aaron controlled his pitches, even in a full count? That boy's father sure must be proud."* He closes his eyes. *"That* boy's father."

"You had some good plays, too," I say. "You threw that runner out at second. That's a hard throw." I politely omit the fact that it was during practice.

We are both looking out into the backyard, not saying anything. The redbuds are coming out on the trees, and daffodils are coming up along the backyard fence. I turn my face to the sun, letting its warmth fill my face.

"You wanna throw a little?" asks Sean. "I could use some practice catching."

"You want me to pitch? To you?"

Sean shrugs. "Sure. I'll practice blocking and dropping."

The dig is not lost on me. "Shut up." And then, "But I can't play too long. I still have to work on my history paper." I never did turn in my draft to Ms. Rowe, and the final is due next week. Ba said he would take me to the library.

After Sean gets his gear, we practice in the backyard. For a moment, it is not Sean in front of the hydrangeas—it's Nelson. Nelson squatting down, Nelson flapping his glove at me, Nelson tossing the ball back. My chest hurts for a moment at the memory, but then it eases, a rough stone becoming smooth.

I'd forgotten how much I loved to throw—and throw hard—to hear the snap of the ball in the catcher's glove. I'd forgotten about that great split second between the windup and the delivery, unloading all that coiled energy.

"You're not bad," says Sean. "Why haven't you pitched?"

I stop in the middle of my windup. I spin the ball in my hands, trying to come up with a good answer. "It hasn't been the right time."

"If Erin leaves the team, you'll definitely have to pitch."

I shake my head. "Nah. There are others." But I am avoiding the real question. Erin. And my mom. When I think about my mom and Erin, the whole problem starts to chase itself in a circle.

· CHAPTER ·
TWENTY-NINE

WHILE I'M AT THE LIBRARY, I LOOK UP ERIN'S ADDRESS in the phone book. There's only one Nickelson in our town. She doesn't live far—a ten-minute bike ride away from my house.

After thinking of lots of different possibilities, I've come up with one possible way out; Erin offers to leave the team. That way, Ba doesn't ask her to go, and the rest of the team would remain. *You're putting the team at risk*, I imagine saying to her.

Unfortunately, my brain doesn't have time to make this a solid plan before Erin answers the door.

"Hey," she says.

"Hi." We stare at each other through the screen door. It is the same voice, same face, but a completely different person.

"Erin? Who is it?" A woman comes to the door, wiping her hands on her apron. "Is this someone from school?"

"It's Peter, Mom. From the team."

"Oh." Erin's mom bobs her head awkwardly. "Hello, Peter. Do you want to come inside?"

"We'll go sit in the backyard," Erin tells her.

Erin's backyard has a rail fence, and as soon as we walk back there, Erin climbs on top of a rail and straddles it, like a horse. "Did your dad send you to kick me off the team?" Her tone is very matter-of-fact, but she doesn't look at me when she asks.

"What? No!" The stoutness of my answer surprises even me. "Ba wouldn't do that. Send me, that is."

"So . . ." Erin hesitates. "Are we going to play?"

In those few words, I hear the longing in her voice, the yearning that doesn't want to be there. I try to couch my words as gently as possible. "I don't know that, either," I admit.

Erin swings her legs up so that she can stand on the top rail, a feat I have tried on other fences and never quite achieved. She puts her arms out for balance. "So what are you doing here?"

I try to start the conversation I meant to have. "Some of the kids are threatening to leave the team if you stay."

"I know." Erin jumps to the ground. "Who?"

"Bobby, Jimmy, and Coop," I say. I feel a little guilty saying their names. "I mean, it's really their parents."

"Wow," says Erin. "Bobby and Jimmy, you can take 'em or leave 'em. But Coop. Losing him would be bad."

I have to smile, just a little. Even at this point, Erin can't stop thinking about the game. "You know, you make it sound like if only the bad players threatened to leave, it wouldn't be so terrible." I walk over to the fence so she has to look at me. "But the thing is, the team needs to have at least nine players. You know that." I wait, not saying any more, hoping she'll get the hint.

"And if I stay, there won't be nine players."

"Not by my count."

Erin lets out a long breath. "My dad told your dad that if he wanted me to leave, to just tell us."

"Except my dad won't ask you to leave. He says it's not fair."

Erin puts a hand on her hip. "Darn straight it's not fair. I'm as good a player as anyone on that team. Better. You know that."

"I know. But if you stay . . ." Erin only needs a second to figure out where I'm going.

"You're asking me to *volunteer* to leave, aren't you?"

I can't look at her when I answer. "Yes."

Erin says the next words slowly so I can understand each one. "You want me to give up baseball."

I cover my head with my hands. "Look, if there was a way to keep playing and have you be on the team, I'd be all for it. But I can't see it working out."

Erin is shredding the wooden rail with her fingernails. "Well, I'm not. I'm not going to make it that easy on you. You're going to have to kick me off the team." She turns to look at me. "Did you really think I would just walk away?"

Of course I didn't—not really. Because I couldn't leave the game, either. Even when I thought I had left, it stayed with me. It's become what I hold on to in my hardest moments. It must be the same for Erin.

"I'm sorry," I say, getting up. "I made a mistake. I shouldn't have asked."

Erin takes my apology easily. "You had a weak moment. It's been known to happen." She lifts her chin. "Did you bring your glove?" It's her way of asking if I want to play catch.

"Nah. And I should get back."

"Didja hear that President Nixon is getting involved in the baseball strike? That's how important baseball is. The president of the United States gets involved."

"I hadn't heard that."

Erin walks with me to my bike. "So what's going to happen?" she asks.

"I think that if the president of the United States wants baseball, they'll figure out a way to make it happen."

"Not the strike, dummy. *Our* team."

"I don't know," I say. "If it were up to us, we'd play, right? You'd stay, and there'd still be a team."

"Of course."

Of course. It's just not as easy as it sounds.

·CHAPTER·
THIRTY

AFTER A FEW DAYS OF HEARING FROM EVERYONE, BA has called for a meeting at five.

I ask in the car what he has decided.

Ba looks away and shakes his head slightly. I don't know what that means. *No*, I'm not letting Erin stay on the team. *No*, I'm not going to tell you.

No, no, no.

"What do you mean? Is Erin staying on the team?"

"What do you think should happen?"

"We should play," I say simply.

"But what if that means Erin gets kicked off the team?"

I won't make the decision my father wants me to make. "*You* should be the one to decide. Not me."

Ba doesn't say anything for a minute. Then he says, "Let's see what happens at the meeting."

I think of all the times Ba told me what to do, saying, *I'm your father; you must listen to me.* And now the one time I want him to tell me what to do, he won't.

. . .

We get to the field about fifteen minutes early, and other people show up early, so that by the time it is actually five o'clock, most of the team is there, gathered around the bleachers.

Erin and her dad are the last to arrive. Everyone stops talking when we see the green station wagon pull into the parking lot, and we all watch them walk toward the field. They take their time, not making eye contact with any of us.

When they reach the bleachers, Mr. Nickelson raises his head and looks at a couple of the other dads. "Warren, Eli," he says. "John." No one says anything back, though I do see Doug's dad nod his head slightly. Erin looks up, too, at me. Her eyes are wide, questioning. I think of all the times she looked at me from the mound, looking for a signal.

I don't know what to wish for, or what to think.

"I would like to thank everyone for coming today," says Ba. He stands, facing the bleachers, his back to the field. We all turn in his direction, away from Erin and her dad. This is the first time he's talked to all of us, parents and players. He holds up a clipboard, reading from a piece of paper.

"I have heard from many of you, expressing your

opinion about whether we should keep Erin Nickelson on the team. Some of you have told me that girls should not play baseball, and Erin should not be on this team. I cannot say that I agree with everyone, but that is to be expected."

Ba clears his throat and keeps reading. The paper curls around the edges, as if it has been folded and carried around for a long time.

"I know many people who like the game of baseball very much. They would probably even say that they love the game. Most of these people are boys and men. They like to play the game and read about the game and watch the game, and when they are not doing these things, they like to talk about the game or collect the baseball cards."

I cringe a little when Ba says *the* baseball cards, but a few of the dads laugh and nudge their sons, not to be mean, but because they are the ones Ba is talking about.

Ba flips the paper over and keeps reading. "The world is changing, though. Women are becoming doctors and lawyers, policemen and truck drivers. And some of them are baseball fans. Some of them enjoy this game as much as anyone here, know as much about the game as any man or boy."

Now some of the dads and players look at Erin. Of course, they are thinking that Ba is talking about her, maybe just her. But Ba could have been talking about Mom, too. This time last year, Mom was still telling everyone about the game she saw at the new Three Rivers Stadium.

"It seems to me," continues Ba, "that there are many reasons why someone should not play baseball. If they cannot have good grades, for instance, or keep up with their schoolwork. But a good reason is not whether someone is a boy or a girl. As we have seen on our own team, a girl can play just as well as a boy, if not better."

"You're making a big mistake," growls Mr. Lattimore. He is wearing a dark blue jacket that has LATTIMORE TOWING stitched on the back, and he has big, meaty hands. Ba looks small compared to him, like model trains built on a different scale. Some of the other dads murmur their agreement with Mr. Lattimore.

Ba holds up a hand. *Wait*. "I said I had an opinion. And you have been kind enough to listen. But I have decided that this is not my decision to make." Ba swallows and lowers the clipboard.

My heart jumps. What is Ba doing?

"So we're going to take a vote?" "What is this?" "Is that fair?" The voices of the parents begin to rise and clash with one another. This is exactly what I was afraid would happen. Chaos. Confusion. Anger.

Ba raises his hand again. "Someone once told me that you have to be the change you wish to see in the world. And as parents, we often want to make these changes for our children. But this time, I think the team needs to make the decision. *They* need to decide what kind of team they want to be." Ba draws in a breath.

Be the change you want to see. The words echo in my head. Oddly familiar but out of place at the same time.

"All I ask from each player is that this be *your* decision, not your father's or mother's decision. Yours. And I will abide by it." Ba lowers his head.

"You want the children to decide?" says one of the parents. "What kind of decision is that?" Some of the players make low, angry sounds. We're not *children.*

"It's their team," says Ba simply. "It's their game."

The whole group falls silent. The sun casts long shadows in the dugout, and the shadows move only slightly as all the players trade glances. Some of them, Sean and Rickey and Coop, look at me. *Did you know about this?*

No, I want to tell them. *He didn't tell me.*

No one moves.

Maybe Ba will stand alone.

. . .

Sean is the first one to stand up and walk over to Ba, followed by Doug and Yonder. Rickey glances over at his mother for a second, then makes his way down the bleachers and over to the growing group. Mrs. Torres makes a clucking noise with her tongue, but says nothing. Erin puts her head down and scoots near Ba, her ponytail now swinging down her back. Someone mutters, "That figures."

Then the flow of players stops. No one else goes over. We are stuck between two half teams, like a bridge too short to reach the other side. I glance at Ba, wondering if he had considered this possibility.

And then it hits me. Maybe there is an answer to this.

It's as though I'm seeing all the players for the first time again, and I can see everything about everyone: Coop is shifting his weight, the way he does right before a batter takes a swing, and Sean is rubbing his hands together 'cause he's excited. Even Martin is there, glove in hand, thunking a ball into the pocket.

Glove.

Around the bleachers, I see all the players have brought gloves. Even some of the dads. Everyone wants to play. *I* want to play.

Then my feet are moving under me, and I am walking toward Ba, because this is the answer. And I know who told Ba about being the change you wish to see in the world, who Ba must have been thinking about when he was talking about people who love baseball.

All this time he has never said his name, never talked about him directly. But Ba hasn't forgotten him. He is just remembering him in a different way.

Nelson.

I turn and face the remaining players. "C'mon," I say. "Let's just play ball."

Coop crosses and uncrosses his arms and then walks over quickly, like he's afraid he's going to change his mind. I hear someone whisper, "Yes." I think it might be Sean.

Bobby and Jimmy look at each other.

"I was going to pitch this season," says Jimmy.

"Was not," says Bobby.

"Was too," says Jimmy. "*Am going* to." He sticks his chin up in the air and walks over to us.

Bobby peeks at his father.

"She'll ruin the game," says Mr. Lattimore. "Mark my words."

"We've got eight," whispers Doug. "We just need one more to play."

"She hasn't ruined the game so far," says Bobby.

I look at Martin and Bobby. Martin's parents are not here—he rode his bike to the field. No one is making Martin come. He wants to be here.

"Think you're up to pitching two games in a row?" I ask, loud enough for Martin to hear.

Before Erin can respond, Martin rolls his eyes. "Oh, c'mon," he says. "They need help, obviously."

Martin strides over to the group, like he had always planned it that way. But in a blink, I see him look at my father and nod his head, and my father nods back.

Bobby is the last one to join us.

"That's it?" says Mr. Lattimore. "Just like that, you're going to keep playing?"

"Every player had a chance to make their own decision. It looks like the team would like to stay together." Ba crosses his arms and raises his chin.

"You'll regret this."

"It is possible," says Ba. "But right now, I would like to focus on having a practice."

The whole team is staring at Mr. Lattimore; he is the intruder now, holding us up. Mr. Lattimore walks away, shaking his head. Other parents are drifting away. It doesn't matter. Right now they are outside the boundary, outside of where our team begins again.

·CHAPTER·
THIRTY-ONE

JIMMY PICKS UP A GROUNDER FROM BEHIND SECOND and tosses it, underhand, to first. To Erin.

Erin catches it and throws it back. Hard. "The runner is coming, Jimmy. You have to *throw* it. Not act like you're at an egg toss."

Jimmy ducks his head. He didn't have this problem when Coop was playing first, before Erin rotated in. He also spends a lot of time looking over there, even when the play is not there.

"Are you afraid of hurting me?" Erin demands. When Jimmy shrugs and looks away, not denying her charge, Erin shakes her head in disbelief. "This is *me*, remember?"

"I'm trying," responds Jimmy. He lifts up his cap and wipes his forehead. "I'm *trying*."

Jimmy's not trying hard enough, though. After a few more egg tosses and missed outs at first, Erin whips the ball back so hard Jimmy takes his hand out of the glove and shakes it.

Rickey, on second, covers his mouth with his glove. "You better start making that play, man. You are making her *mad.*"

Jimmy shakes his hand out again and doesn't say anything. And on the next ball that comes to him, he throws the ball to first, hard.

Our team is working on getting to normal again, which means trying to play the way we always did, while remembering that Erin is a girl, but then remembering that it doesn't matter that Erin is a girl.

Like all things in baseball, it takes practice.

The funny thing is, it's easier for me when Erin and I are talking. You'd think it would be easier to not think about Erin-the-not-boy at other times, but it's when we talk baseball that everything seems to go back to normal.

"How about this one," says Erin. "Two outs, runners on second and third. Batter knocks it out of the park, but no runs score."

"No runs? Not one?" I'm stalling for time.

"Not one." Erin crosses her arms and grins.

"And the batter, he doesn't do anything stupid like just stand there?"

Erin shoves me. "The batter could be a *he* or a *she*, but no, the batter does not just stand there."

I have a feeling that there is an answer to this, but I have to take a stand. "Can't happen."

Erin spreads her hands wide. "Runner on third fails to touch home. Not touching the base means that the runner who was on second touches home first. That creates the third out, negating any additional runs."

I nod. She got me. "That's a good one." And then, before she gets too full of herself, I think of one. "Do you know who the first commissioner of baseball was?"

"No-o-o," says Erin. "Should I?"

"Kenesaw Mountain Landis," I say, savoring the sounds of the words.

"You're making that up."

"If I were going to make up a name, you think I'd make up *Kenesaw Mountain Landis*?"

Erin laughs. "Good point." She looks down. We're actually standing on top of home plate, talking. "You know, I never noticed this before, but home plate actually looks like a little house."

She's right. Home plate has five sides, shaped the way a little kid would draw a house. From the catcher's position, though, the house is upside-down.

"I think that's just a coincidence," I say. "They don't call it home plate because it's shaped like a house."

Erin sighs. "But it's even better that way, don't you think? Like it was meant to be that way?" She opens her arms and lets them fall. "It was home before anyone knew it was home. That's what I love about baseball."

Erin may play like a boy, and even talk baseball like a boy, but sometimes she says sappy things like a girl.

"And it's called a bat because they used to use real bats to hit the balls," I say. "You'd hold them by the feet and then get them to extend their wings . . ."

Erin shoves me. "But you know what I mean, right?"

I'm tempted to tease her some more, but I don't because even if I don't say it, I feel the same way she does. Part of what I like about baseball is that there are rules, and then there are mysteries and possibilities within the rules. Like getting to first base on a third strike, or a no-man triple play. Or peanuts on radios.

"Yeah," I say. "I do."

. . .

When Ba and I get home from practice, something amazing happens.

"The strike is over," Mom tells me when I walk into the living room.

For a moment, I think I'm going to fall over. Not because the strike is over and the season is going to happen, but because Mom is actually starting a conversation with me. And it's a conversation about the outside world, the world beyond us and this living room.

Mom gestures to the TV. "They just announced it."

"Wow," I say, trying to keep things light. "Finally. When do they start?"

"In a few days. The Pirates are going to play at Shea Stadium."

In the Before, we would have been dancing around the living room, I'm sure. But now I am standing and she is sitting, an awkward space between us. I'm almost afraid to come any closer to her, as though I might break some fragile space around her.

Then I think of Erin. *Practice.* We'll practice.

I sit down on the couch, as close as I dare. "Who do you think they'll start at pitcher?"

Mom doesn't say anything for a moment, and I wonder if I've blown it. Then she surprises me.

"It's gotta be Dock." Dock Ellis.

I close my eyes, taking in the moment. "What about Steve Blass, though?"

"His ERA last year was pretty good, but Dock's was a little bit better," says Mom.

Laney comes in and sits between us. Part of me is jealous of how easily she slides in next to Mom. "What are you guys talking about?" she asks.

"The strike is over," I tell her. "There's going to be a baseball season."

"Who, your team?"

"No, no. The Pirates. All the teams in the major league went on strike, but now they're going to play."

Laney thinks a moment. "But you. You were never going to not play, right?"

It takes me a second to parse Laney's question. "It's hard for me to not play."

Laney giggles. "And it would be hard for Mommy to not watch baseball."

I look at Mom, who smiles faintly but doesn't say anything. I wonder if Laney means the Pirates or my team, and I wonder what my mom thinks she means. But I don't ask because I just want to let the possibilities be out there.

·CHAPTER·
THIRTY-TWO

WHEN I WALK INTO HISTORY THE NEXT DAY, MS. ROWE calls me over. I can tell she is excited because she is bouncing up and down, and the fringe on the bottom of her shirt bounces with her.

"Peter," she says. "Look at this."

It's my paper on an aspect of Franklin Delano Roosevelt's presidency. I actually worked kind of hard on this, to make up for not turning in a draft. For my topic, I picked Roosevelt's "green light" letter. Nelson had told me about it once, but I researched it some more. I even found a copy of the letter on microfiche at the library.

At the beginning of World War II, Kenesaw Mountain Landis wrote to Roosevelt, asking if baseball should be suspended because of the war. Roosevelt wrote back the next day, saying that he thought it was best for the country that baseball go on, so that people would have a form of recreation.

In other words, baseball shouldn't stop because of the war; because of the war, it was important for baseball to keep going.

At the top of my paper, she had written *A+* and circled it. A note next to my grade said, *I knew this was the work you were capable of.*

"I'm so proud of you, Peter," she gushes. "This is first-rate. I never knew this about Roosevelt before. It's a great example of how Roosevelt kept up morale during the war."

"Thank you," I mumble.

"From now on," she says, "I'm expecting *all* of your work to be of this quality. Have you started thinking about what you might write about the Korean War?" That is going to be the last war we study in class.

It only takes me a moment to come up with one. "Did you know that Ted Williams actually led the American League in hitting after serving in the Korean War?"

Ms. Rowe thinks about it, and then wrinkles her nose. "Maybe your topic should be a little more central to the actual Korean War."

"Okay," I say. And I mean it. "Okay."

After dinner, I head over to Folger's Lot with my glove, hoping to join a game.

There's only one other person there, though. Chris. He sees me before I can walk away.

"Where is everybody?" he asks me.

"Beats me." Then I add, "I know they're not at a Pirates game. Yet."

"Yeah, well, that couldn't be over fast enough."

We both stand there awkwardly, searching for something to say. Just as I wonder if I should make up an excuse to leave, Chris asks, "Wanna throw?"

We start about fifteen feet apart, gradually moving away from each other as our arms get warmer.

"Did you hear about Ms. Rowe?" shouts Chris, as he launches the ball toward me.

"No. What?" I jump up to catch the ball, but it sails over my head. For a minute, I think he's talking about Ms. Rowe's chat with me today in class.

"She's getting married."

I run to get the ball. Chris must know this because his mom substitute teaches at the school. "Oh, okay." I throw the ball back. No wonder she was in such a great mood today.

"You haven't heard the best part." Chris neatly fields the ball I throw to him. "She's not changing her name. She's still going to go by Ms. Rowe."

Now I get it. "Gunderson's head is going to explode."

"*Boom!* Like an atomic bomb. I think her eyes will pop out first," suggests Chris.

I can almost see it—the moment Miss Gunderson finds out that Ms. Rowe is still going by Ms. *and* keeping her maiden name. We'll probably have pop quizzes for days, maybe a twenty-page paper. "No, the top of her head will pop off first," I say with the authority of a medical expert. Then I add, "Ms. Rowe's not so bad."

"My mom says we should be grateful people are still getting married, and not just moving in together . . ." shouts Chris.

We stay at the field and throw and talk and throw. Chris tells me that he and Melissa kissed behind the Minute Mart after sharing a box of candy Bottle Caps.

"And?" I ask.

Chris shrugs. "She tasted like root beer."

I decide to tell Chris about Erin. Chris isn't fazed at all.

"World's kind of a messed-up place, you know? There are bigger problems than girls playing baseball."

I nod. Chris is right: The world *is* messed up. But then, we have baseball. Baseball reminds us that there are still good and joyful things in the world, even when times get bad.

Friendship does that, too. Even friendships that have gone off the rails for a while.

"Come back tomorrow?" I ask Chris.

As Chris and I walk home, I look over my shoulder to see the sun set over the field. The sky is dark, stained orange and purple at the edges. The streetlights have come on; one light stands over home plate, casting it in a yellow light.

At the far edge of left field, there's a figure walking toward the trees. I can just make out the details from where Chris and I are. Dark hair. Blue jacket. He carries something long and thin.

Like a Louisville Slugger bat, with red tape on the handle.

This time, no one pulls on my elbow to disrupt my vision. I watch the person fade into the darkness among the trees. He moves with a slow purpose.

It could be anyone, but I choose to believe.

· CHAPTER ·
THIRTY-THREE

ERIN IS LATE TO WARM-UPS. IT'S PROBABLY JUST AS well—the less time she's on the field, the less time the other team has to figure out that something's up. Some of the guys suggest, only half-jokingly, that we stick her out in right field, which is the position farthest away from the Panthers' dugout.

When Erin does show up, she looks different. It doesn't take long to figure out why.

"You cut your hair?" I say, remembering at the last second to lower my voice. Her braid is gone. Short tufts of hair stick out from under her cap. It's not boy short, but it's not super long, either. I look over at the Panthers dugout, to see if anyone is looking at our latest player, but no one seems to care. Maybe it's true what Erin said—people only see what they want to see.

"Lots of guys wear their hair like this," she says. "My mom says the unisex look is really in right now."

"You cut off your hair," says Sean, with some admiration. "That's dedication to the game."

When Jimmy sees Erin's hair, though, he is less excited. "Guys have long hair, too!" he says. "You could have pretended to be a guy with long hair."

Erin gives Jimmy a look. "So you want me, a girl, to pretend to be a guy who looks like a girl?"

Jimmy grins. "When you say it like that, it sounds more complicated."

"It's not a big deal," says Erin. She lowers her head, and runs her fingers through the bits of hair at the nape of her neck. But her fingers keep going after her hair has stopped.

We are almost done with warm-ups when Sean comes racing onto the field. Even though we haven't started the game yet, his hair is plastered to his head and little trickles of sweat run down his face. Sean motions for us to come into the dugout.

"What's going on?" asks Rickey.

Sean leans over, pressing his hands into his knees. "The other coach said he heard we had a girl on our team. He said he'll pull his team if he finds a girl."

I look over at the other dugout, and realize I know who the other coach is. It's Dan Bennett, from the tryouts.

"It's a forfeit if he does that," says Doug. "We'd get the win."

"Aw, wins on forfeit are cheap," says Martin.

We all turn and look at Erin. We hadn't considered what would happen if someone was actually looking for her.

"What do you want to do? You want me to leave?" she says.

"You're supposed to pitch today," I remind her.

"As much as you fooled us, I think the coach might be able to spot you on the mound if he's looking for a girl," says Martin. "Like a sitting duck." He shakes his head. "My arm's still pretty sore from the last game. I don't think I can pitch another game today."

"I could pitch," offers Jimmy.

"A whole game?" asks Martin. "Against these guys?"

Jimmy falls silent. He's not ready, and he knows it.

"Besides, we still gotta stick Miss Baseball somewhere on the field," says Martin, jerking his thumb at Erin. "We only have nine." Bobby is out sick.

I pull off my catcher's helmet and pads to cool off. I hold them in my hand, feeling their heft. An idea begins to form in my head.

"Erin, you could catch," I say. "Put this gear on and no one's the wiser."

"Can you catch?" asks Martin.

"Ask my two older brothers," says Erin. "I don't like it, but I can do it." She takes the helmet out of my hands and jams it on. Once she adds the chest protector and the shin guards, it is a pretty good disguise.

Ba walks in. He looks at me, out of catching gear, and then looks at Erin. We tell him what's going on. If Ba is at all rattled by this development or the prospect of not exactly telling the truth, he doesn't show it. "So who's going to pitch?"

This was the harder part of the plan I've concocted. I pick up my glove, my regular glove, and say, "I am."

The pitching mound feels a hundred feet high. And I pitch like it, too. I throw the first two warm-up pitches over Erin's head, and the third one into the dirt. Erin stands up and jogs over to the mound.

"Just relax," she says. "Get the ball over the plate."

"It's been a while," I mutter. "I'm a little rusty."

"We're playing catch, okay? You can do this."

But I can't stop thinking. I'm thinking of what will happen if we get caught. I don't want to have come this far to lose it all again. I'm thinking of Mom. I'm thinking of what Nelson would say, and what hydrangeas look like in August.

I know what he would say. *Don't overthink it.*

I am in the middle of the windup when Ba walks out with Dan Bennett. I can't help myself. I stop the windup and pretend to study the ball so I can hear what they are saying.

"It's a bit hot," he says. Mr. Bennett is taller than I remember, though his voice is the same. "But we should have ourselves a fine game."

Ba nods. "We are looking forward to it."

I hold my breath. They are only a few feet away from Erin. I make a wish for them to finish talking and go back to the dugouts. *Go go go.*

"Just one more thing," says Mr. Bennett. "There's a rumor going around that you might have a girl on your team, Mr. Lee." He points a thick finger at Ba. "If that's the case, I will pull my team, with the full backing of the league's board of directors."

It's hard to believe that I ever wanted to play for Dan Bennett.

Erin stays perfectly still, crouched in the catcher's position.

Dan Bennett takes a few steps into the field and looks at each player. "You," he calls to Doug in right field. "Come here."

Doug has longish dark-brown hair that curls around

223

the edge of his cap. He jogs across half the field before Coach Bennett shakes his head. "Never mind," he says. "Darn kids with their long hair."

He turns his glare to me. I let him get a good look. "That's my son, Peter," says Ba.

"Figured as much," says Coach Bennett. "Not too many Orientals around here, you know."

I throw Erin a pitch so she can look busy. The ball hits the plate, but Erin drops down and blocks it. She picks up the ball and throws it back to me.

For a moment, I fantasize that Ba will grab Mr. Bennett by the front of his shirt and tell him to leave our team alone.

Instead, though, Ba points at Erin. "Our catcher. Our catcher is a girl."

Erin's look of shock must mirror my own. I think we're both going to be sick. Ba and his truth telling. But suddenly Bennett throws his head back and roars with laughter. "Oh, you got me," he says.

"I got you?" asks Ba, unsure of the phrase.

"Well, sure. C'mon. If a girl was going to play, she sure as heck wouldn't play catcher. You'd stick her in the outfield and pray that nobody hits to her." He turns to Erin. "What's your name there?" he asks.

"Erin," she replies, not looking up. I cross my fingers and hope that he doesn't ask her to spell it.

"Nice block," he says. "Oh no, that's no girl. No one out there but fine young men." He claps Ba on the shoulder. "See, I knew that rumor didn't make any sense. I told my wife that you Orientals understand this situation. You're traditionalists. Girls belong in the kitchen."

Ba turns slowly so that Mr. Bennett cannot see him give me a long look.

"I certainly agree," says Ba. "That *girls* belong at *home*."

I almost collapse right there on the mound. And even under the catcher's mask, Erin's smile is impossible to miss. As soon as Ba and Coach Bennett walk away, she holds up her glove and then signals one finger, straight down.

Fastball.

I hurl it in, as straight and fast as a ray of light.

"I think Erin's braid was good luck," says Jimmy. It's our last at bat, and we're down, 6–1. One out. Coop's at bat. Rusty's pitching has been as good as advertised.

"It's not like we won all our games before Erin cut her hair," points out Doug.

"I know," says Jimmy. "But we need . . . *something*."

"Like what?" says Sean. "Snacks?"

I know what Jimmy means. It's not the score; it's the mood in the dugout. I jump up and grab the fence. "Coop, Coop, he's our man! If he can't do it, no one can!" My voice sounds thin all by itself and I feel kind of silly, but it does the trick. The pitcher throws it outside. The count evens up, 2–2.

"C'mon," says Erin. "Everybody, get up!" She joins me at the fence and Jimmy and Bobby follow. Our voices grow stronger, until we're shouting, "NO ONE CAN!"

The pitch is low. Coop starts to swing, and then stops short. Check swing. We hold our breath. The ump hesitates half a second, and then calls a ball. Full count.

We all draw in a deep breath and then start screaming again. "Coop, Coop, he's our man . . ."

CRACK! It's a beauty—a long arcing hit, behind the center fielder. Coop makes it to second—a stand-up double.

Now it's Doug's turn. Rickey's on deck, Erin's in the hole. If we get that far, I'm after Erin. We're yelling so much and so loudly that the words become strange stretched-out sounds.

Doug swings late and the ball dribbles off the edge of the bat. For a second, the pitcher and the catcher can't decide who's going to get it, which is enough time for Doug to land safely on first while Coop makes it to third.

Runners on the corners, and one of our best hitters coming up—Rickey. We're about to start cheering when Martin interrupts us.

"You're just going to keep doing . . . that?" he says. "For everyone?"

"We've gotten two hits in a row, and now we have a runner at third," says Erin. "You don't mess with a streak. Chanting is our streak. Everyone knows that, right, Rickey?"

Rickey thinks about it, adjusting his batting helmet. "Call me Rick," he says, after pausing a moment. "My sister's best friend is here today."

Ooooooohhhhhhh, the rest of us croon back to him, but *Rick* ignores us. We get through two rounds of *Rick, Rick, he's our man* before he slaps a single into center. The center fielder catches it on the bounce and throws it to second, getting Doug. Coop comes home.

Erin's up. And now there's some controversy over whether we can do the chant that says Erin is *our man*.

"We could do that one where you spell the name . . ." says Jimmy.

"No! We have to spell it the girl way," says Sean.

Erin looks back at the dugout. She's not in the batter's box yet because we haven't started chanting.

"Oh for Pete's sake, you guys are a bunch of morons. This isn't rocket science." Martin stands up and walks over to us. Then he grabs the fence and starts shouting.

"Extra, extra, read all about it!

Erin's gonna smash it!

No doubt about it!"

"There," he says, stalking back to his seat on the bench. "Now you have a chant for *Erin*."

I scan our opponents' faces, checking to see if anyone cares that we've changed our chant. No one seems to care about that. They do, however, seem to care deeply when Erin hits one into the gap and Rickey makes it home. 6–3.

Now the team is chanting, "Two out ral-ly!" I'm up. I've had a single and a walk so far. When I reach the plate, the team switches to our new chant.

Extra, extra, read all about it!

Peter's gonna smash it!

No doubt about it!

The pitcher scowls at me; I'd be mad, too, if a rally started while I was pitching.

Ba tells me to swing away, and I'm thinking I'll lay off the first pitch, figuring that the pitcher will go with something off-speed. When the pitch comes in, though, it's just ripe for hitting, right down the middle of the plate. It's crazy because it's like everything is going at one-tenth speed. I can see the stitches, the Rawlings stamp, the stain of grass on one side.

When the bat connects with the ball, it feels like the ball is soft, like hitting a wet sponge. I don't even have to look—I know it's gone. There's a pop the bat makes when you hit it well. I can hear the oohs, even from the other team, and I see the pitcher throw his glove on the ground. Out of the corner of my eye, I see the ump twirl his finger.

Nelson had told me about this—I hit the sweet spot of the bat. "When you hit the sweet spot, there are no rattles, no bone shakes," he said. "It's like everything's so perfect, it all moves together."

As I pass first, my legs feel the way they did when I went ice-skating the first time—not when I was actually skating, but after I'd taken off the skates and was walking across the locker room. Freed of the weight of the skates, my legs felt weirdly light, and I wasn't actually sure my feet were touching the ground.

Erin waits for me at home and we jump on each other, screaming our heads off. We're within one run of tying the game. But more than that, it's because we love this game. We love this game.

It's Martin's turn to bat, and for a moment, all the screaming stops and both teams watch Martin in silence. He's the tying run. Martin knocks the dirt off his cleats.

"Don't get out," says Coop quietly. Martin glares at him.

Martin goes into his stance, the tip of his bat making tight circles. Martin swings at the first pitch. Strike. You can hear the other team sigh with relief.

"What are we doing?" Erin squeaks, jolting us out of our daze. "C'mon! Keep up the streak!"

For a split second, the dugout hesitates. It's Martin, who was just complaining about the cheering.

But no, you don't mess with a streak.

We start screaming. "Extra, extra, read all about it. Martin's gonna smash it . . ."

Martin goes to full count. He fouls off one, then two more. We scream louder. The pitcher draws himself up, nods at the catcher, and goes into the windup.

There are three sounds.

The first is the grunt from Martin as he takes a swing.

The second is the "huh" from the umpire, calling the third strike.

The third is the sound of the ball crashing into the backstop.

Complete silence. Then it hits me. "First! Run to first!"

The batter becomes a runner when the third strike called by the umpire is not caught . . .

"Pick up the ball! Pick up the ball!" screams the other coach. The catcher scrambles briefly, and then makes a wild toss to first. The ball sails over the first baseman's head. Martin tags first and takes off for second.

"What's he doing?" wails Doug. "They're going to nail him. He should just take first."

The right fielder scoops up the ball and sidearms it to second. He throws wide. The second baseman stretches for it, but the ball goes just past the tip of his glove. The ball shoots into the outfield.

"He's still going! He's still going!" screams Jimmy.

Martin barrels for third. Everyone on the Panthers side screams at the fielders to just hang on to the ball, "Eat it!" But the temptation is too much. The right fielder launches a cannon to third. Ba is already signaling for Martin to stop at third. Two hands, palms out.

The third baseman has to leap up to catch the ball. He comes down with the ball, but as soon as he hits the ground, the ball pops free. Erin and I look at each other, and I know what she's thinking: *A third-strike home run!*

The loose ball is all the encouragement Martin needs to head for home, seventy feet from a win. He blows by Ba and his sign to stop. We're all screaming, *"Go go go,"* as if our voices can make him go faster. "Go, Martin! Go!" There's no stopping him now. It's going to be decided at the plate.

The catcher is a big kid, bigger than Martin, practically as big as Ba. He hit a triple during the first inning. He sets up in the base path, straddling the path. The ball arrives a split second ahead of Martin.

"Knock him down!" yells Erin.

"Slide to the outside!" yells Sean.

But Martin does neither. Instead, he twists and slides, slipping between the catcher's feet. A thread through a needle. His feet touch the base as the catcher tags him on the head.

We hold our breath.

The umpire pauses a moment, and then jerks his hand back. "You're out!"

For a second, our team deflates. A collective "nooooo" fills the dugout, and I see Martin's head flop back down to the ground.

It's over.

Around me, I can hear the mutters of why and suggestions of what might have been. Sighs. And the thing is, part of me knows I *should* feel disappointed. But a lightness springs in my chest, as happy as a balloon, so that all I can do is laugh. It bubbles out of me and floats up.

I was wrong, wrong to wait for a winning game. That's not what my mom loved, and, I think, still loves, about the game. More than winning, it's the game itself, and people playing it to the limit. That's what it has to be.

Rickey turns around and gives me a strange look. "He said *out*, Pete. You know that, right?"

"I know, I know, but . . ." I gesture toward the field. "C'mon. That was . . . just . . ." I try to organize my thoughts as Martin trudges into the dugout.

"Shoulda stayed on third," gruffs Martin. He gives me the hairy eyeball. "Don't know what *you're* so slap-happy about."

"Martin," I grab him by the shoulders. "You were

going to score on a *third strike*. You had to try. I mean, it would have been great."

"But I *didn't*, so it *wasn't*."

"Well, scoring a run would have been better, but just trying was kind of . . ." I pause, trying to find the right word.

"Spectacular," suggests Erin.

"Amazing," agrees Coop.

"Comical," says Rickey.

"It was interesting," says Ba, who is standing by the dugout entrance. At the sound of his voice, we all freeze, wondering if Martin is going to get into trouble for not listening to Ba. Martin takes off his cap and coughs. There might have been a *sorry* buried in there.

"I suppose we should work on baserunning" is all Ba says.

"Let me guess," says Martin. "Forty laps."

· CHAPTER ·
THIRTY-FOUR

MARTIN WAS WRONG—WE DON'T RUN FORTY LAPS AT the next practice.

Instead, we play Over the Line and Pepper, the games we had played at Folger's Lot. We run relay races, with one team starting at home, and the other at second, holding bats over our heads as we run. Ba doesn't know the names of the games, but when he tells us the rules for a game, we usually know the name.

"We have one batter, one pitcher, and everyone else is the fielder. When you catch a fly ball, it is your turn to hit," says Ba.

"Hey—that's Catch-a-Fly," Rickey tells him.

Maybe Ba knows the game by another name in Chinese, but he just isn't telling us. At first, everyone kept looking at me, as if maybe I knew that my methodical Ba had been replaced by a fun-loving alien life-form, but after a few minutes, it's clear that we are still practicing. To keep hitting in Catch-a-Fly, you either have to hit the ball on the ground, or try to hit the ball so hard and so far that no one can catch it.

Instead of letting the ball drop between them, the players in the field vie to see who can make the most spectacular catch. When Erin makes an over-the-shoulder basket catch, everyone else tries to do it, too. Bobby dives for the ball, rolling over and over into the dirt. Coop lays himself out flat to snag a line drive in a play that's worthy of any major leaguer.

Sean hits a blooper toward Martin at first. Martin sets himself under the ball when, at the last second, the ball is snatched away.

"Hey!" shouts Martin. "Give it." Martin has been waiting for his turn at bat, and has not hidden his impatience.

The rest of the field starts chuckling.

Martin turns around to see who has stolen the ball, and finds himself staring into Ba's face. Martin takes a step back and puts his hand on his chest in shock. "You can't go around scaring a guy like that!" It is the first time I've ever seen Martin admit he is scared of anything.

Ba flips Martin the ball. "You can still bat. But you should call for the ball."

"You shouldn't sneak up on people," responds Martin. Then he bends over and puts his hands on his knees as Ba walks away. "I didn't think the old guy had it in him," he says to no one in particular. "He really surprised me."

That makes two of us.

Ba and I are the last ones to leave because we need to rake the field and pick up the equipment. Just as we are getting ready to leave I see Ba raise his hand and begin waving. A blue car, kicking up dust, heads toward us.

It's Liao *Su Su*. He parks the car and gets out. "Hey!" he says. "I just saw you from the road." He smiles widely and shakes Ba's hand. Liao *Su Su* and Ba begin speaking in Chinese, trading the usual beginning-of-conversation pleasantries. *How are you? Is this where you play baseball? How have you been?*

I am beginning to tune out when I hear the car door open and close again.

It's Clarissa.

It's Clarissa, who is the same, but not. She still has long hair, but now it's really shiny and straight. Silky. She brushes her hair out of her face.

"Hi, Peter," she says, kind of shy.

"Hi," I say. My throat feels thick. "Clarissa."

Maybe it's a trick of the low-lying sun that's making her look this way. Kind of golden and lit up. Her eyes look different. Did she wear glasses before? I can't remember. Or maybe it's the dress she's wearing, which is royal blue and short. Above-the-knee short.

She doesn't look like a stick anymore.

"We were driving by, and my father saw you all and said we should stop," says Clarissa. "I told him it looked like you were leaving, but he didn't listen to me."

I look at the ground so I won't keep staring at her. "That's okay," I mumble. Suddenly I have this weird thought that it would have been nice if Liao *Su Su* and Clarissa had come by earlier, when I was pitching really well.

"You look different," I say. "Did you used to have braces or something? Glasses?"

"No-o-o." She draws out the no so it goes up and down, like a musical note. I suppose she could have been insulted by my question, but she just looks amused. "I heard you were playing baseball," she says. "And your dad was coaching."

I nod and try to think of something interesting to say. "We have a girl on the team. She's really good." I hear the words coming out of my mouth, though it feels like they bypassed my brain completely.

"I heard that, too." Clarissa turns her head, so that her hair spills over her shoulder. A vocabulary word pops into my head: *cascade*. "That's cool. My dad says that your dad said that the team was going to break up over having a girl on the team, but you convinced them to stay."

What? Why would Ba say something like that? "Oh, no. It was my dad, really. He did that."

"Clarissa! We should go," says Liao *Su Su*. "Your mother is expecting us."

Clarissa turns to go. And then she stops. "Maybe it wasn't either one of you. That kept the team together, I mean."

"Huh? Then who was it?"

A lot of people say that smiles go *across*, but with Clarissa, her smile also goes *up*, so that her eyes smile, too. "Maybe it was both of you," she says, right before she gets into the car.

I remember when Nelson told me that *one day* I would understand about girls, that I would understand what it meant to have a beautiful girl look at you and want to sit next to you. *One day* is here, and I wish Nelson were here. He would laugh and say *I told you so*. And then I would tell him that *one day* something else happened—that Ba and I worked on something together. I think that would have surprised him even more.

• • •

When Ba and I get home from practice, Laney is riding her scooter on the sidewalk. She runs up to me as I get out of the car, and she smells like laundry that's been dried outside—wind and sun and dirt all mixed up together.

"I saw an oriole today. A Baltimore oriole," she says.

"That's one more for your life list, huh?" I say.

"Did you have a game today?"

"Just a practice, but we had fun. Our next game is Saturday, I think."

Laney smiles. What I don't tell her is I don't know how many more games we'll play. Maybe we'll finish the season, or maybe someone will figure out Erin at the next game. But we'll play, that much I know. As a team. We might play in the league, or maybe we'll just play Catch-a-Fly and Pepper on a lot that hasn't been mowed in two weeks. But we were meant to play.

Ba gets out of the car. "Elaine, Peter—go inside and wash your hands. We should have dinner soon."

But none of us heads inside right away, not even Ba. Even though the sun is getting low, it's still warm. It's a spring evening. The birds are calling to each other and the trees and grass take on a soft glow.

I grab Laney by the arm, and put a baseball in her hand. "Hey Laney, throw me the ball."

Laney holds the ball awkwardly, bending her arm so that her hand is by her shoulder. "Why?"

"Trust me. You're gonna love this. It's better than bird-watching," I promise.

Laney twists her lips and raises one eyebrow. "*Better* than bird-watching?" she asks skeptically.

She's stalling, so I go back over and show her what to do. How to bring her arms straight out, like a scarecrow, but with her head turned over one shoulder. The way Nelson showed me a long time ago.

I walk about fifteen paces away, turn, and face her. "Just throw me the ball." I don't really expect her to get it to me exactly, but that's what she does. A perfect chest-high toss.

"Hey!" she says. Her face is a perfect O of surprise, her mouth and eyes wide open. "I did it!"

We toss the ball a few more times. She catches the ball on her second try, putting her hand on top of the ball the way I told her to, so the ball won't pop out.

"This is *kind of* fun," she says.

Ba steps in, and we make a triangle. Since I'm the only one with a glove, I toss it gently to Laney, she throws it to Ba, and then he throws it harder back to me.

Maybe baseball is in our blood. We're just meant to love this game.

Maybe, just maybe, it's time. It's time to stop waiting.

I go to the living room doorway and take a deep breath. I want to ask now, before dinner, while it's still daylight.

"Mom," I say.

She is lying down on the sofa, covered by a blanket. She might have been sleeping, though the TV is on, set to a low hum. She turns her head slightly.

I walk over and kneel down so that our heads are close together. No one else needs to know what I'm going to ask. It can be just the two of us.

"Mom."

Her eyes flutter open. When they focus on me, she lets out a long breath.

"My team, my baseball team," I say.

Mom slowly raises herself up. I keep talking because I think maybe my words are pulling her up.

"We're good, and we're having fun, you know? We—me and Erin—we're playing good ball," When I say Erin I realize that Mom may not know about Erin and everything that went on, so I add, "Erin is a girl. Ba let a girl on the team. She's a pitcher."

Mom nods slightly. "I know. I know about Erin."

If Mom knows about Erin, maybe she's ready.

I put my hand on her arm. "Mom, I'd really like you to come to one of my games." Then I hold my breath after the last word, so I don't miss anything she says.

Mom looks past me, over my shoulder.

"It's really beautiful right now, too," I say. "It's great baseball weather."

Mom gets up and slowly walks until she is halfway across the room. She is staring through the doorway at the kitchen window. I get up, too, keeping a few steps back. If she takes half a dozen steps, she'll be at the window. The window is open, and she might be able to smell the lemon-vanilla scent of the magnolia. If she takes a few steps beyond that, she'll be at the back door.

Maybe, she'll remember. She'll remember what it's like.

Mom lifts up one hand, and folds it over her mouth. Her head moves, just slightly, side to side.

"You could come for part of a game. Just a little bit. You could see me pitch." I hate begging, but I can't help myself. "And have an at bat."

Mom shakes her head, harder this time. "I'm just not ready, Peter."

I'm not ready to give up. I put my hand on her arm.

"What about just sitting outside, Mom? Can we just sit outside, on the step?"

It's hard to believe she'll say no to such a beautiful evening. But maybe that's exactly why she says no—it's just too beautiful to bear.

· CHAPTER ·
THIRTY-FIVE

I AM SITTING ON THE BACK STEP, ALONE. FOLDED UP, chest against the tops of my thighs, because I am pretty sure that in any other position, I will fly apart. I am just holding together. Every breath I take tests how far I can go, the limits of how tightly each piece of me can hold on to the rest.

I do not know how long I have been like that when I feel a hand on my back. It's Ba.

"Peter? Elaine told me you were here. Are you okay?"

Out of reflex, I say yes. But then I shake my head. No. Ba wrinkles his forehead. He asks if something happened.

I could tell him the whole story, my whole plan about playing, to make Mom feel better. But that doesn't make sense, now that I know how it ends. So instead, I tell him the last thing that remains from this whole mess.

"I wish Mom would come to one of the games," I say. It's such a simple statement, but I am laid bare by its honesty.

"Mommy's not feeling well," said Ba. "You know that." Ba is the only one left in the house who calls Mom *Mommy*.

"But she should. She should come to a game. I'm pitching, I'm catching. We're all hitting. *You're the coach.* She loves baseball. What else does she want?" My voice rises until it cracks, and I bang my fist against the concrete step until it scrapes my skin. "Why do I even have to ask?"

Ba lowers himself next to me. "I do not know, Peter." There is an ache in his voice that I have not heard before, and I remember what he always said about Mom—he knew he wanted to marry her when he heard her laugh.

And then I do tell him my plan. I tell him about the one good day. The best day. The day I've been living on for the last six weeks, and how I'm trying to get another one.

"I mean, I'm just saying, I thought that if we had some really good things to talk about, she might feel better. And I thought one of those things would be baseball," I say. "If we won a game. And I even thought, sometimes, it was working."

"It might be working," says Ba, not unkindly. He presses his fingertips into the bridge of his nose. "I wish we could make her feel better."

I have never heard my father wish for anything. All things are supposed to be attainable through effort and hard work. But to him, I suppose, you wish for the things you cannot work for.

"I don't know what to do next," I say.

Ba lowers his head and clears his throat. "What you do is keep moving. Some days you will only do small things all day. You get up in the morning and you get dressed and you wash your face. You go to school. I go to work. We have baseball."

As he speaks, I realize this is exactly what my father does, what he has been doing for the last seven months. Small things, but the things that have kept us going.

Then Ba adds, "And other days you can lift your head, and do great things."

"Like letting Erin play," I say.

"Like letting Erin play," says Ba. "Or deciding to play at all."

Suddenly, a hummingbird, bright and red, hovers a few feet in front of us. It cocks its head toward Ba, and then me. I can feel a small breeze from the whir of its wings. Its bright black eyes make me think it knows something even humans don't know.

For a moment, the ache inside me subsides. Elaine

would love to have a hummingbird on her life list. I turn to call to her, but then the hummingbird flits away.

"What are we going to do? About Mom, I mean."

Ba stares out into the yard for a moment before speaking. "Peter," he says. "Will you always be a Pittsburgh Pirates fan?"

"What?" I am startled by his question. "Yes. Of course."

"Even if they have a very terrible season?"

That is hard to imagine; the Pirates won the Series last year and the National League East two years ago. "I'm no fair-weather fan."

"What if they have many terrible seasons?"

"I'm still a fan," I say resolutely.

"You will not give up?"

"No." Ba's questions are beginning to annoy me. "I already said that."

"Why? Why won't you stop?"

I lift my hands for a moment, partly in frustration, partly because I'm searching for the right words. "Well one, because that's what a good fan does. You're loyal to the team. And two, because there's always next season. You can always hope they'll do better the next season."

Ba looks at me and does not speak until I understand. I must wait. As long as I have waited for Mom, I must wait some more, even when it's the last thing I want to do.

Ba stands up. "Come," he says. "Let's go inside."

"No," I say stubbornly. "I'm staying here. Maybe I'll stay out here until she comes out." I know the words are childish, even as I say them, but I don't care.

"That's not reasonable," says Ba.

I stay on the step. Ba sits back down next to me and waits. In the Before, he would have ordered me inside. But not now.

"It's the Pirates' first game of the season at home," says Ba after a few minutes. "We could go inside and listen."

This is enough to jolt me.

"You never listen to games," I say. If anything, Ba had always made a point of reading his newspaper in the kitchen while Nelson, Mom, and I listened in the living room.

"I will listen today," said Ba. "*We* will listen to the game today—you, me, your mother, and Laney. We do not have to leave the house for that."

In this statement, I find just a little bit more patience. Enough to hang on to.

Ba reaches over and unfolds my fist, placing something small and bumpy inside.

It is a peanut.

I stare at it for a moment, not quite believing what I'm seeing. A peanut. The radio. The Pirates. "Who told you?" I asked. "When did you know?" I rub my finger over the top, where the little bump for opening the shell is. Because you have to show that you believe.

"Your brother told me," said Ba. "And always."

Your brother. Always.

Nelson once told me that baseball is different from other games because it has no time limit. You could go nine innings, but then you could go fifteen innings. Twenty innings. That's when you find out what the team is made of, which ones have the stamina and the guts to hang in there.

The ones that keep having hope. Always.

Ba turns to go inside. And this time, I stand with him.

Our home, our family, won't be the same as it was. It never will be.

But we can be the ones who keep having hope. My family. Together.

AUTHOR'S NOTE

This book was born from several inspirations, near and far.

My first inspiration came from around the world in the form of Taiwan's twenty-plus-year dominant run of the Little League World Series. Beginning in 1969, the teams from Taiwan so heavily dominated the sport (winning ten times in thirteen championships) that the teams were accused (and eventually cleared) of cheating, and at one point, international teams were banned. These teams were a high point for Chinese-Americans like my parents, who grew up in Taiwan after fleeing China's Communist takeover. In the 1970s, Taiwan faced a series of international frustrations, as the United States turned from its support of Taiwan to mainland China, and these teams were a very bright spot during a generally dark time.

While I have no memory of them, my family joined countless other Chinese-Americans in their summer pilgrimages to Williamsport to support the Taiwan team (often known as Chinese Taipei). In a family that emphasized academics, taking the time to make this journey was quite notable. I am not aware of any other time that my family attended or watched a large-scale sporting event.

There was, however, one other exception to my family's generally lukewarm stance toward sports. In the early 1970s, my brother played baseball in Wilmington, Delaware, and, because there was a need for a coach, my father agreed to coach the young team. From this situation came my second inspiration: At some point, a girl asked to play on my brother's team, at a time when girls were forbidden to play baseball by rule and social mores. My father was inclined to let her play, but a few parents on the team threatened to pull their sons from the team rather than let them play with a girl.

My father came up with what I thought was a wonderfully thoughtful solution. In a letter to the boys (alas, lost in a move), my father urged the boys to consider that the roles of women in the world were changing, and told them that the decision to play or not was ultimately theirs, not their parents'. When all was said and done, not a single boy left the team, and the girl finished the season with the boys. (Notably, during the week I was putting the final touches on this story and exactly forty years after girls were permitted to play Little League, Mo'ne Davis became the first girl in Little League World Series history to pitch a shutout.)

I have always loved this story about my dad. My father and I did not always see eye to eye in my youth, perhaps because he had grown up in war-torn China and I was raised in the safe confines of suburban Washington, DC. But this story told me so much of what he thought was possible for me, and his sense of justice in the world.

During the late phases of this story, I discovered a wonderful account of various sandlot games in America on the website www.baseballplayamerica.com, edited by Donald Weiskopf and his wife, Anne. The growing tension between kid-led sandlot games and more formal Little League type play, as described on the site, is one that I found fascinating; while many good-hearted and talented adults devote countless hours to the sport, I often wonder if some of the joy of the game was lost when adults came to control so much of the play. Donald and Anne have graciously allowed me to reprint their account of the games here, with the mutual hope that these games may once again find a place in the American childhood experience.

Revival of Baseball Pick-Up Games

By DON WEISKOPF, publisher of Baseball Play America

Many years ago, during the summer, in the afternoons following school and on weekends, youngsters made the neighborhoods reverberate with the sounds of playing games in parks, vacant lots, and in the streets. Among the many games were stickball, scrub, over-the-line, wall ball, strikeout, and later on, wiffleball. There were always 3 or 4 of us to play some version of a game. . . . If kids didn't have enough players for stickball, they would play Army Ball, "Catch-a-fly and you're up. . . ."

Ever mindful that the large majority of young kids today do not play pick-up games, nor do they and their parents know how, the following low organized games are a few of those that young children used to play. . . .

WALL BALL

EQUIPMENT: *A wall with a drawn strike zone, rubber or tennis ball, and home plate.*

DIRECTIONS: One or more players stand about 20 to 40 feet from the wall, preferably concrete. The game begins by having each player throw a ball against the wall. As a drill, throws can be fielded by the player who made the throw. As a competitive game, a player other than the thrower has to field the ball and the "pitcher" can vary the type, speed and difficulty of throws. Rules can be established as to catching the ball on a fly or a bounce. . . .

ARMY BALL

EQUIPMENT: *Hard rubber ball and bat.*

DIRECTIONS: This popular West Coast "stick" and ball game often involves three players, a pitcher, batter and fielder. Of course, more players can play. As to how the game got its name, the field was spread from any makeshift backstop to any tall building, barracks, whatever. This was strictly a pull-hitting game. Batters cannot hit the opposite way. If the batter hit the building above one level, it is a double, another level a triple, and the roof and over, home run. There are no walks in Army Ball. The batter stays at bat until he hits or strikes out. This serves to make hitters wait for desired pitches.

OVER THE LINE

EQUIPMENT: *Ball and bat.*

DIRECTIONS: Referred to also as Line Ball, this is a favorite playground, school and yard game. With two teams 30 feet apart and perhaps 6 players on a team, the object is for the batter to drive a ground ball through the other team. Each team has a bat. The first player tosses the ball up and tries to bat it across the other team's goal line. The ball must hit the ground between the two lines. The other team tries to field the ball and then attempts to bat it back across the opponent's goal line. Each member of each team gets a chance to bat. One point is scored for each ball that crosses the other team's goal line. Another variation is for the players to throw rather than bat the ball. . . .

CATCH-A-FLY AND YOU'RE UP

EQUIPMENT: *bat.*

DIRECTIONS: One player is at bat and the rest of the players are in the field or down the street. When a fielder catches a fly ball, he gets to hit. Most kids will come up to the plate swinging, trying to hit a home run or a hard line drive. Some will hit a few on the ground so they will stay up longer. So a pitcher may want to throw high pitches to make the batter hit flies. Rather than be close behind the plate, the catcher will position himself safely farther back. If he catches a pop fly, he may be allowed to hit.

PEPPER

The batter stands about 15-20 feet away from a fairly straight line of fielders. Batter hits grounders to the fielders, fielders field the ball and pitch it back to the hitter and on and on. Many rule options. Hitter can lose his turn if he lines out or fouls off more than a couple balls. Fielder can become the hitter by catching a pop out. Fielder can be eliminated by making an error . . . This is a great game for bat control, fielding, throwing strikes, etc.

THREE FLIES UP

This is a simple game where either someone pitches to a hitter or the hitter just tosses the ball to himself and hits until someone in the field catches 3 pop flies. That fielder then becomes the hitter. A variation might be to [award] certain point totals for fielding different balls. For example, 10 points for a fly ball, 5 points for a ball on one hop, 2 points for a grounder. First fielder to a certain number wins or gets to hit. . . .

OVER THE LINE—VARIATION

A field is set up with an area for the hitter. Then, a straight line is established about where second base would be, then another where shallow right field would be. The width of the field is determined by how many people are in the field. The hitter either tosses the ball to himself or hits a pitched ball into the confines of the field. If it lands to the left or right of the boundaries he's out. A ball that makes it past the first line on the ground is a single. If it lands in between the first and second line in the air it's a double. If it goes over the deepest fielders head, homer. Outs are made by fielding any grounder in front of the first line or catching a ball in the air. Three outs switch. . . .

—————————————————————————

Game contributions from Brent Mayne

ACKNOWLEDGMENTS

A second book, it turns out, is just as daunting as the first, and I am so grateful to have so many wonderful people on this journey with me. My writing group saw the early draft of this story, and gave me the encouragement to stick with it: Jacqueline Jules, Moira Donohue, Marty Rhodes Figley, Marfé Ferguson Delano, Anamaria Anderson, Liz Macklin, Suzy McIntire, Carla Heymsfeld, Anna Hebner, and Laura Murray. Madelyn Rosenberg probably never wants me to use present tense again, but she'll have to take this one— thank you for getting me over the finish line.

I count my lucky stars every day to have a second book with my ever kind and wise editor, Lisa Sandell. Thank you also to Jennifer Ung, Starr Baer, Emma Brockway, Saraciea Fennell, Antonio Gonzalez, and the rest of the Scholastic family for sharing your talents with me.

Quinlan Lee and Tracey Adams of Adams Literary provided me with guidance, assurance, and good humor at every step of the process—thank you! Bill Nixon, a neighbor and baseball coach, generously shared his expertise on youth pitching with me. I am also grateful to have visited the Peter J. McGovern Little League Museum in South Williamsport, Pennsylvania; I found many helpful details there that I incorporated in this book. And I would be remiss if I did not mention the 2012 Washington Nationals, who taught me what it is to love a team.

At the heart of everything I am able to do is my family. I am blessed to have a mother who told me, "You can do anything," a father who expected me to be in the game and not on the sidelines, and a brother who challenged me. My husband, David, is my rock—his encouragement and support are as boundless as the sky, and I cannot imagine doing this without him. Our three children, Matthew, Jason, and Kate, keep me on my toes, make me laugh, and remind me to dream. Love you.

ABOUT THE AUTHOR

WENDY WAN-LONG SHANG is the author of *The Great Wall of Lucy Wu*, which was awarded the Asian/Pacific American Award for Children's Literature, and *The Way Home Looks Now*, an Amelia Bloomer Project selection and a *CCBC Choices* selection. She is the coauthor of the forthcoming novel *This Is Just a Test* and lives with her family in suburban Washington, DC.

IF THE SOVIETS DON'T BLOW US UP, MY GRANDMOTHERS JUST MIGHT.

David Da-Wei Horowitz has a lot on his plate. Preparing for his upcoming bar mitzvah would be hard enough even if it didn't involve trying to please his Jewish and Chinese grandmothers, who argue about everything. And he's trying to dig a fallout shelter with his friend Scott . . . who doesn't want to let David's other best friend, Hector, come along.

Dual identities, dueling friends . . . David's life is about to go nuclear.

COMING SOON FROM WENDY WAN-LONG SHANG AND MADELYN ROSENBERG!

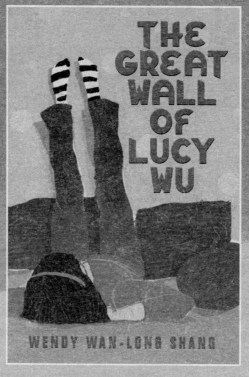